THE RED BRA

Jenny Middleton

ISBN 978-0-9985671-3-6

Heron Porch Publishing

THE RED BRA

THE 9TH ERA

Prologue

Once upon a time, there was a Red Bra. She had two sisters. At times she adored them, at times she was ashamed of them, at times she flaunted them, and at times she hid them. But nonetheless, they were her sisters, and they were here to stay. Until...

Chapter 1
New Year's Eve

The late afternoon sky was bedazzling with its hues of red and gold shining across the Pacific Ocean as the sun slowly made its descent towards the horizon. Besties since High School, the trio belted out the lyrics to "California Dreaming" while admiring the view as they drove north on Highway 101. The excitement they felt as they headed for the premiere New Year's Eve event was almost palpable. Excited to have another semester completed at UCLA and finally reaching the magical age of twenty-one, they cheered while driving into Santa Barbara. They giggled with child-like abandonment when the majestic hotel appeared before them. They parked under the portico, and the valet opened their doors. Getting out of the car, they looked around in awe at the ornate details adorning the massive glass doors to the entrance. The bellhop instantly appeared and gathered their suitcases and hangers which held their evening attire. A red bra was looped over one of the satin covered hangers and resting atop a sparkly red blouse. As the bellhop began to hang the festive clothing on the cart, a strong wind whipped through the portico. Captured by the breeze, the red bra was lifted by the wind and silently slipped from the hanger's crook and fluttered in the air. The bra's owner gasped in utter dismay to see her bra sailing through the air for all to see. She chased after the wayward bra and reached out her hand only to merely graze the satin strap. The strength of the winds increased, and the red bra soared upwards to the heavens. Suddenly, and without warning, the gale force winds ceased, and the red bra began to take on a life of its own.

Freedom! RB cried. *Oh, blessed freedom! No longer am I strapped to my sisters. Whoo-hoo! I have a world to explore and explore I will!*

The sun continued to cast its golden glow across the horizon on that magical day, New Year's Eve. A day when old acquaintances shall be forgotten and never brought to mind.

Time ceased to have meaning as RB drifted through the gentle breezes savoring her new-found freedom. No one tugging on her cups or tightening her straps. No sisters peeking out of her cups and embarrassing her in their attempt to show off their plump curves. She held onto the wind and reflected on her days that were spent giving support which wasn't always appreciated. She felt such utter freedom no longer encasing the melons of her past.

I want to go back to my youth! she cried out to the rising sun. *Back to the days when my job was to support, to be uplifting, to – to just be.*

The soft breeze shifted, and RB found herself gently floating downward ever so slowly and growing smaller, smaller, smaller....

Chapter 2
5th Grade PE Class

"Geez, get a load of her," Riley mumbled to one of her besties, Julia, while nodding towards Sophia.

"Eww," Julia grimaced, having seen Sophia pull off her frilly blouse and thrust her bra covered breasts in their direction. "Can't she just change into her PE clothes like a normal person instead of like a stripper, geez," she whispered to Riley.

Giggling, Riley held on to her gym locker door and rested her face against the cool metal.

Sophia stared at the girls while chatting nonstop to no one and everyone about the new bra her mother bought her. "Yeah, I have one to match every outfit I own. I almost wore the scarlet one today, but I chose the mauve one because, well, it blends better with my new blouse and... oh, Riley – you STILL don't have a brassiere?"

Riley turned her back to Sophia and quickly pulled her Aeropostale T-shirt off, briefly exposing the tank top she wore beneath. Swiftly, she pulled her PE shirt on over the tank top before slamming her locker shut and shooting a steely glance at Sophia.

"Ha ha, you haven't passed the pencil test yet, have you?" Sophia sneered.

Biting her lower lip, Riley bent down and tied her shoes, determined not to give Sophia the satisfaction of a response

Well, la-de-da. I do believe if push came to shove it would be discovered that Riley has more that needs a bra than Sophia! Flatsies, flatsies, they're flatsie's cuz they're flat! RB shouted unheard through the stagnant locker room air, willing the gods to let Sophia hear her. *Just who does that little tart think she is with her matching brassieres at eleven years old! My, oh my, I can see her future now.* RB threw back her straps and laughed. *I'm sure there are plenty of poles just waiting for her to disrobe on.* RB straightened herself and hovered above.

Riley ran her hand through her short cropped dark hair and stared down the length of her thin torso and muscular legs. *Who cares about a stupid pencil test anyway*, she silently muttered as she left the locker room and joined the class in their warm-up laps.

Chapter 3
Riley

Riley jumped from the top of the three short steps to the concrete landing at the entrance to the girls' locker room. She was glad another boring day of school was over, and she could do what she loved, basketball. Her best friends, Sydney and Julia, raced in after her. She was glad Sophia wasn't on the team and briefly thought about the taunts she threw at her about not wearing a bra. *Yeah, like any other fifth grade girls wear bras,* she thought to herself while turning the dial on the combination lock on her locker. *At least I don't think they do. Geez! Why do I care?* She pulled her practice clothes from her locker and stripped off her t-shirt for the second time that day, exposing the tank top she wore beneath.

"Gawd, did you see what Lily did to Joey in the hall today?" Sydney asked. "She is such a jerk. I mean really!"

"I think she likes him," Julia quipped as she pulled off her Nascar t-shirt exposing her tank top beneath. Riley took note that like her, Julia didn't wear a bra either.

"I know!" Sydney exclaimed, "She's always pushing him into the lockers, and she never gets in trouble for it!" Sydney turned her back and pulled off her Justin Bieber T-shirt. Riley noticed she was wearing a white bra.

"Sydney," Riley said, not sure why her voice rose an octave when she spoke, "when did you get a bra?"

"Oh, Mom got me some when school started. They feel kinda weird, but Mom said boys might start looking at me, and I need to be covered. I don't know what she meant by that, and I can't imagine wearing one of these every day!"

Julia and Riley walked over to Sydney to take a closer look at her bra. "So, does it bug you?" Julia asked.

"Not really, but I like tank tops better. Oh, my god, did you hear Sophia at PE? Like she has anything that needs a bra!"

"I don't think I ever want to wear one," said Julia. "I don't think I ever even want boobs!"

The girls cracked up with laughter, threw their arms around each other and strode out of the locker room.

Hmmpf, maybe I have been blessed by always being with grown-up girls. RB thought, processing the scene that was just played out in front of her. She adjusted her cups and let the wind lift her and sweep her upward. She floated along the gentle breezes surveying the scenery below. She basked in the glow of the sun as its last rays of the day shone upon the land in their muted colors of pinks and yellows. RB continued to digest the scene she had witnessed in the girls' locker room

Don't ever want to wear one! She mimicked Julia's response to owning a bra. *Oh my, so much these young ladies need to learn! If only they knew of all the options out there! Why, there are cotton bras, satin bras, sport*

6

bras, underwire bras, padded bras, water bras, push-up bras, wonder bras, shelf bras, nipple-less bras… Oh my, did I just say that? RB smirked, recalling some of her sister bras. *Training bras! That's what these young ladies need. At their age, it's not about the support; it's about modesty, fitting in, and being confident so they can grow up to be proud of their bodies!*

With that thought, RB once again adjusted her straps and flew off in search of her budding young girls.

***

"Mom," Riley said as they were clearing off the dinner table. "Can I get a bra?" Riley's mother laid the dish towel down and turned to look at her daughter.

"A what?" her mother's right eyebrow formed an arch, and she briefly studied her daughter's face.

"A bra. Ya know, to wear under my clothes," mumbled Riley, now embarrassed that she asked.

"Good grief, Riley, you're barely 11 years old! What do you need a bra for? Turn around, let me look at you," she said, lowering her eyebrow and squinting her eyes. "Hmm, you barely have buds. Trust me; bras are uncomfortable, don't rush it."

What! RB cried in disbelief, arriving at Riley's home in time to hear her mother's comment. *Well, she obviously has never worn my brand, or such nonsense would not fall out of her mouth. Who is she to thwart Riley's notion of bras before she ever wears her first one! Doesn't she realize what a tender age this is?*

Riley lowered her head and finished clearing off the table. She knew better than to argue with her mother. Since her parents' divorce, she could barely talk to her mother without a fight erupting. *I don't need a stupid bra anyway*, Riley thought before walking to her room. Grabbing her phone, she hopped on her bed and texted Julia.

what up?

workin on this stupid math hw

Yeah, m class stinks

did u no S had a bra?

Idk, mayb I don't look at girls boobs LOL

U want 1?

I hv 2 LOL

u hv 2 bras?????

no – boobs!!!!!

I think we need bras

I think I need to finish my math ttyl

THE RED BRA

Riley stared at the phone. *What's her problem?* Riley wondered. *Since when did Julia want to do math homework instead of text?*

Oh my, RB snickered, absorbing the scenario below her. *To bra or not to bra, that is the question they ask – rah rah!*

Riley put her phone in its docking station and cranked up the One Direction playlist she and Julia had downloaded together. Staring at her phone, Riley mulled over their conversation. Lifting the phone from its station, she paused the music and poised her thumbs over the keyboard. But instead of texting, she tossed it to her bed where it bounced once before flipping on its back. *Why text her again?* Riley thought. *She's acting too weird. Heck, she doesn't even like math!*

Riley walked to her dresser and scanned the remnants of her young life scattered across the top. A miniature Strawberry Shortcake doll her daddy gave her when she was four years old was leaning against the mirror on her dresser. A Casper the Ghost Pez container her grandmother gave her at Halloween was resting in a bowl of hardened tootsie rolls that her braces prevented her from eating. Tiny rubber bands and multi-colored rubber band bracelets lay scattered throughout. Riley picked up a red and white bracelet. She stretched it over her slim fingers and released it to rest on her slender wrist. Aimlessly, she plucked the rubber bands, creating a soft 'ping - ping' against her skin. She continued to survey the memories of her young life. A picture of Sydney, Julia, and herself sitting on the porch swing at Sydney's house, a movie stub ticket from *Catching Fire*, and a box of Ice gum. A small tray with a picture of the Golden Gate Bridge etched on the bottom sat off to the side. It held a pen that contained a clear liquid with glitter in the top. Next to it was a pencil with tiny dog faces wrapping themselves around it, barrettes, and a few coins. Riley picked up the pen and see-sawed it back and forth, watching the glitter flow around the words, Fabulous Las Vegas, which was etched inside the clear tube. Her mother brought it back for her after one of her girl trips. Riley sighed while watching the glitter move ever so slowly, trapped amidst the goo encased pen.

Mom sure is different since she and dad got a divorce, Riley thought as she laid the pen down, her fingers brushing against the doggie covered pencil. Absentmindedly, she rolled the pencil back and forth with the tip of her finger as her mind wandered back to the good days when she saw her daddy every day, not every other weekend.

Riley picked up the pencil and grinned at the tiny Yorkshire, Chihuahua, poodle, and boxer faces staring at her with their tongues protruding ever so slightly out of their mouths. As she rolled the pencil in her hand, her mind skipped back to PE class and Sophia making fun of her and saying she couldn't pass the pencil test.

Riley stood up straight and gazed intently into the mirror. Her large brown eyes stared back at her. She tapped the pencil on the edge of her dresser. Tap-tap-tap. Slowly, she lowered her eyes down the mirrors length following the line of her thin neck and across to her shoulders. She paused as she assessed her shoulders. *They don't look quite as pointy as they did last month,* she thought, *but the neck, yeah; the neck is still way too skinny.* She scrunched her neck down and rested her chin against her chest while simultaneously raising her shoulders. "Gawd! I'm acting like a turtle," she said to her reflection in the mirror as she gave up trying to fatten the look of her neck. She stood straight, threw her shoulders back, and with a deep breath she let her eyes drop a few more inches down the mirrors length, and she stared at her chest.

Barely buds! Seriously, did my mother really say that? She fought the urge to text Julia again while she continued the rhythmic tap-tap-tap of her pencil against the dresser's edge. She lifted the pencil and noticed her tapping had created a dent in a Chihuahua's forehead.

Oh, what the heck, Riley thought, laying the pencil down and pulling her T-shirt off. She dropped it on the floor where it landed on yesterday's discarded socks. She leaned in closer to the mirror, her tank top hugging her slender frame.

I have more than just buds, geez.

She stood back and furtively looked around her room while wiping her clammy hands on the hem of her tank

11

top. She straightened the slats on the closed blinds on her window before walking to her door and making sure it was securely shut. Pressing her body against the door, she wished for the umpteenth time her mother would allow her a lock. "Whatever," Riley mumbled while walking back to her mirror. With one last glance at the closed window blind, Riley flung off her undergarment, threw her shoulders back and proudly stared at herself in the mirror - daring the reflection to mock her. *Buds, ha! As usual, Mom knows nothing about me. These buds are becoming flowers. Beautiful, round, chrysanthemums ready to spring forward and bless the world with their beauty,* she said as she giggled and spun in circles, laughing at how witty she was.

That's my girl, RB beamed with delight as she watched Riley spin in circles, her short hair bouncing joyfully. *Be proud! You are becoming a woman! Let's hear you roar!*

Riley stopped spinning and tentatively placed her right hand on her left breast. She gently cupped it in her palm before lightly squeezing and feeling the hard lump which had begun to form beneath the soft, supple skin. *I AM becoming a woman!* Riley proudly thought. *Now... this stupid pencil test.* She couldn't help but remember when her older cousin, Becca, told her about the pencil test. She and her Aunt Joan had flown in from Iowa during spring break, and they stayed with them for a few days. Riley smiled, remembering how awesome Becca was. Her glance shifted to the barren floor beside her bed. She closed her eyes and held them shut tightly until she could picture Becca lying next to her bed on the blow-up mattress they bought just for her. Most nights they would whisper and giggle for hours until sleep would finally overcome them. She remembered her saying bras were mostly to make your boobs look bigger, and unless your boobs sagged enough to hold a pencil underneath, you didn't need one for support - just for attention. *I'm still not sure what she meant,* Riley thought as she dropped her head, sadness overcoming her as she realized she would never again giggle into the night with Becca or ask her the kind of questions she couldn't ask her mom. She shook her head to clear her mind of unwanted thoughts and let out a deep breath. Picking up her doggie pencil, she pressed it, Yorkie side facing her breast, under her developing flower. She let go, and the pencil instantly tumbled to the floor. Riley picked it up and slowly twirled it in her hands, closely examining each dog's face. She lifted it back to her chest and rested the French poodle under her obviously not full-grown flower. She quickly slouched over as she released the pencil. It stuck for an instant before diving into the pile of dirty socks and day-old t-shirts that were resting amidst her feet.

Who cares about the stupid pencil test anyway? If Sophia passed the test, I bet she put duct tape on her pencil first. Or on her boobs. Riley grinned at the thought of Sophia with duct tape on her boobs. *Pink and gray camo duct tape,* Riley's grin broadened at the thought.

Oh, I knew there was a reason I liked this budding, little flower, RB mused. *I wonder what Miss 'don't ever want to wear a bra' is doing that's more important than texting. I think I will check on her.*

***

Julia, sitting Indian style on her bed, placed her phone on the nightstand and picked up her pencil and math notebook. She stared at the improper fractions in front of her. "Who cares if fractions are proper or improper or whatever the heck they are supposed to be," Julia mumbled to herself. She started to solve a math problem then paused and looked at her pencil. *What the heck is a pencil test anyway!* she said to herself while tossing her pencil to the side, throwing herself backward on the bed, folding her arms behind her head, and staring at the Nascar pictures taped to her walls. She thought about all the times she and her family had gone to the local track to watch her uncle race. Releasing her arm from behind her head, she pulled her long ponytail around and chewed on her strands of hair. Her eyes fell from the posters to the jeans crumpled in a pile on the floor next to a pair of worn out sneakers and her cherished gray hoodie. *I really should pick up my hoodie,* she briefly thought as her eyes skipped over it and to her dresser and a picture of Riley and her at Chuck E Cheese when they were five years old. She pulled her sodden hair from her mouth and sat up. *Geez, Riley's been my BFF forever. I don't get it. Boobs.*

THE RED BRA

When did things like boobs and bras become part of our talks? Tossing her ponytail behind her, Julia stood and walked to her dresser. Lifting her chin and straightening her shoulders, she looked intently at herself in the mirror. Her faded jeans hung low on her straight frame, and she absentmindedly pulled them up higher only to have them immediately slide down, her hips barely broad enough to catch them. Her t-shirt boasted the school's mascot, the yellow jacket. Julia pulled her shirt tight and leaned closer to the mirror. She observed the uneven lumps in the material below the wasp's stinger. She started to lift her T-shirt when she felt her cheeks burn with the flush of embarrassment. Quickly, she turned from the mirror and bounded out of her bedroom. She ran outside, picked up a basketball, and furiously began shooting hoops. A few dry leaves skittered across the driveway, their crunch resounding through the evening air as Julia trampled over them while running towards the hoop for a lay-up. Fall was rapidly approaching, but unbeknownst to Julia, so was womanhood. She shot hoops until she no longer had thoughts of what it would be like to actually have boobs.

Oh, good grief, 'Missy no bra for me', RB thought while she watched Julia shoot hoops in the fresh evening air. *Get real! You're a girl, soon to be a woman! And for cryin' out loud, I bet you would like a sport bra although I must say,* RB thought as she jiggled her cups, *they aren't nearly as attractive as moi, but then again, we can't all be me! This young lady needs to embrace the changes that are coming over her body and will ultimately enhance her life! I had more fun watching my budding flower with her doggie pencil!* With that, RB flounced through the crisp night air and headed back to Riley's.

***

Riley picked up her T-shirt from the pile on the floor and slipped it over her head, sans tank top. She grabbed her phone and tapped on Sydney's name.

what up

YT- omg J B is sooo cute he's singing BF

TB is doing his hair like JB he looks like a dork

I think hes kinda cute

eww

Riley paused and stared at her phone. *Since when did Sydney think a boy in our class was cute! Yuck, if wearing a bra makes you start liking boys I'm not sure I want one,* she thought to herself as she sent another text.

ttyl mom's hollering

K, c u at school

"Riley Jean!"   Laura, Riley's mother, yelled from the kitchen, adding the 'Jean' for emphasis on her third yell.

"What?" Riley retorted as she checked her shirt in the mirror for signs of pencil testing.

Riley walked into the laundry room where her mother was standing, hands on her hips. *Oh boy, what did I do now?* she thought, approaching her mother.

"Did you forget something?" her mother sternly asked.

Noting the sarcasm in her mother's voice, Riley looked her straight in the eye with just a hint of a glare that the older she got, the more she perfected. "Um... don't think so."

"Don't give me that look," her mother shouted. "You know damn good and well what you are supposed to do when you get home from school. Look, just look - look," her voice rising a decibel with each 'look'.

Riley's eyes followed her mother's perfectly manicured pointed finger. *Fuchsia, I think that nail would be,* Riley thought, staring intently at the nail. *Hmm, she should have a bra like Sophia has to match. I wonder if women match their bras with their nail color, or is it just the panties? I think I saw some matching panty and bra sets in Walmart's flyer. I'll have to check to see what color nail polish the model's wearing.*

Riley's thoughts were quickly interrupted when her mother reached out and grabbed her chin, roughly turning it to face the floor by the washing machine.

"Ow," Riley yelled, startled by the fast action of the hand attached to the fuchsia nails.

17

"Geez," Riley mumbled under her breath.

Schmack, Riley's mother dropped her hold on Riley's chin and swiftly slapped her across the face.

"Don't you use the Lord's name in vain little missy."

"What? All I said was geez."

"Lying will get you nowhere, I heard you say Jesus. I'm not stupid, you know."

Riley briefly touched her cheek and wondered if the color of it now matched her mother's nails or maybe Sophia's bra.

Riley's lips curled a little upward at the thought.

"You think this is funny, do you?" Riley's mother said, her hands now back on her hips.

"Um, no," Riley replied, resisting the urge to reach up and touch her stinging cheek. She attempted to put a serious look on her face so she would not glare at her mother and thus unfurl more of her rage.

Her mother stood erect, tapping her toe.

Riley looked down to her mother's tapping toe and saw Cleo's litter box, with its tiny litter covered mountains of poo scattered throughout. Riley thought they looked like sand castles that had been hit by a wave. She wished a wave could hit her, carry her off to sea, and then get rescued by a mermaid.

Oh, crap, Riley thought. *I forgot to clean the litter box.*

"Umm, sorry Mom, I was going to clean it before bed. I promise I really was."

"Promises, promises, that's all I ever get from you. You learned that from your father, broken promises one after another. *'I promise, Mom, if you let me get a cat I will clean the litter box every day,'* her mother said mimicking Riley's voice. "I think it's damn well time we get rid of that cat."

"Mom, no, please, Mom," Riley begged, "I really was going to clean it today. I just, well, I just had some other stuff to do first."

"What, like texting your friends? I think that could have waited until after your chores."

Riley bent down and quickly opened the cabinet by the dryer and pulled out the pooper scooper and a wadded-up Walmart bag. She hurriedly scooped up the dilapidated sand castle poo piles and dumped them in the bag. Cleo came strolling in and rubbed against her legs as she stood to tie off the bag. Riley bent down and rubbed her cheek against the cat's soft fur, easing the sting of her mother's recent slap. She looked up to her mother, and with tears in her eyes she begged, "Please Mom, I promise, I really promise, I'll keep her box clean."

Riley's mother, eyeing the hand shaped welt that had appeared on Riley's face, turned on her heel and left the laundry room without saying another word.

Oh, Lord, just what did I do to warrant having such an unreliable child, Laura mused as she looked up to the ceiling. *I should never have agreed to that damn cat. I should have let her father be the one hosting a cat and disciplining our child for her lack of commitment to the chores required of pet ownership. Ha, lack of commitment. Like Joel had any idea what commitment meant.*

Laura turned sharply on her heel and marched into the kitchen. After pouring herself a glass of wine from the box in the fridge, she leaned on the kitchen counter with her elbows surrounding the glass. Lowering her head, she breathed in the scent of fermented grapes. She swirled the wine in her glass and raised it to the ceiling in a mock toast to the wine gods. *Thank you, gods, for creating cheap wine for cheap ladies,* she thought while lowering the glass and taking a long drink. *Cheap ladies, yeah I'm one of those alright,* she mused as she swallowed the wine. *That bastard Joel left us damn near penniless, but he sure as hell spoils Riley rotten on his weekends. No wonder she is such a brat for me. The worthless SOB, good riddance I say. He was never committed to our marriage. He thought bringing home a paycheck was all he had to do, and I should wait on him hand and foot because of his financial contribution.* Laura took another swallow of wine, swirling it in her mouth before swallowing. *Ah, those rich bitches have nothing on me,* she smugly thought rocking the remaining wine back and forth in her glass. *I bet if I switched their fancy schmancy wine bottles with my good ol' box of Gallo they wouldn't even know the difference.*

Laura took another long drink, proceeded to the refrigerator, and refilled her glass, before sauntering into the living room. She flopped down on the tattered lazy boy, releasing the handle with her free hand. Her feet flew forward on the footrest, and she expertly balanced her wine glass proud that she did not spill a drop. She picked up the mail that was lying on the table next to her and rifled through the myriad of envelopes which included Dish Network promises of a better deal than cable, hardware ads, and credit card bills.

"Oh, shit," she moaned. *I must have been one ass-hole in a prior life to deserve what I have in this one.* She tossed the pile to the side and took a gulp of wine. *God, I could use a cigarette. Another thing I gave up for Joel. Hell, I'd start up again if I could afford them. Let's see, the things I gave up for Joel: Let's begin with college. Getting preggers ended that dream, and that was definitely Joel's fault.* Laura took a drink of wine and adjusted herself in the recliner. She let out a loud sigh before continuing her reminiscing. They had been dating for a little less than a year. Joel was in his last year of college as a business major, and Laura was a sophomore with an undeclared major. Sometimes she thought she wanted to be an accountant even though math was never her strong point, at other times she contemplated nursing, but blood wasn't her strong point either. Besides, she wasn't much of a people person. Perhaps that was why she didn't mind it when Joel suggested she drop out of college to marry him and raise a family. But now she found it was pretty tough to get a decent job without a college degree. Being a checker at Walmart somehow wasn't what she envisioned for herself in her early thirties.

Taking a sip, she became pensive thinking back to the night she got pregnant. She and Joel had attended a concert on campus. She couldn't remember the name, just that it was a local band doing a free gig to get some publicity. Joel had a flask of whiskey in his back pocket, and they shared sips back and forth all night. Laura was more of a beer and wine girl and didn't anticipate the wobbly legs and slurred speech which overtook her by the end of the evening. Laughing and weaving down the sidewalk arm in arm they walked to Joel's place. He and another guy, Tom, rented an apartment close to campus. They stumbled in and wound their way to Joel's bedroom and crashed on his bed. Joel lay over her and brushed her hair from her face, tucking it behind her ears. He leaned down and kissed her neck. God, she loved it when he did that. She remembered how his neck kisses set her on fire.

Laura shook her head and glanced down at the empty wine glass in her hand. *Time for a refill*. She slowly walked to the kitchen and once again filled her glass. *Another nice thing about boxed wine,* she thought, *you can't tell how much you drank.* She smirked at herself and thought how foolish she had been to have unprotected sex. Somewhere in her whiskey-soaked brain, she knew he wasn't using protection, but she thought, or at least in retrospect, she thinks she thought, it couldn't happen to her. "Whatever," she said a little too loudly before tossing back a gulp of wine while walking back to the living room. A slight smile escaped her lips as she continued to think about the sex of her youth. *That was one area Joel and I never had a problem with. Gawd, I miss having regular sex and feeling sexy.* She thought back to the care she took to wear sexy bras and panties. *My charge card could surely attest to that.* "Ha," she laughed out loud, remembering the fiasco with the water bra. She flopped back down in the recliner and pushed back causing the footrest to rise. Adjusting herself, she sloshed wine on her arm. Leaning forward to lick off the tiny red rivulets racing around her wrist, she thought back to her college roommate, Maggie, and her black lace water bra. She grinned while remembering how when the 'water boobs' were inserted they gave Maggie one heck of a slutty looking cleavage. *That was probably the day we bonded,* Laura thought wistfully.

Maggie was getting ready to go on a first date with one of the guys from the TEK fraternity. Laura was lying on her bed chatting with her while she got ready. Maggie had her back to her as she put on her bra and blouse. Laura was staring at the ceiling, tossing her stuffed rabbit, Thumper, up in the air and catching it. Thumper was an Easter gift from Joel. He used to call her his little bunny. Laura scowled at the memory and took another sip of wine. She remembered when Maggie turned around and said, "Ta-Da!"

Laura turned her head to look, and Thumper the bunny came crashing down on her head. Laura's mouth fell open, and she quickly jumped off the bed and pranced over to Maggie. "Oh, my gawwd! When did YOU get a boob job?"

Maggie laughed and threw her head back, her thick blonde hair bouncing off her shoulders. "Pretty good, huh?" Maggie said. "It's a water bra! Come here," Maggie grabbed Laura's hand and placed it on her breast. "Squeeze – but squeeze gently, I don't want to turn into Old Faithful before my date."

"Wow," Laura said, gently squeezing the water-filled sack. Laura lifted her other hand to feel both breasts at once. "How nifty is that!" she exclaimed, dropping her hands and taking a step backward. "Check out that cleavage, oh my gawwd, it looks so real. Bounce up and down."

"What?" Maggie asked, arching a perfectly plucked eyebrow and looking incredulously at her friend.

"Bounce up and down, you know, I want to see how they act."

Maggie shook her head but obliged and did a few little hops.

"Oh my gawwd, they look so real! Where did you get that? I have to have one, or two, or three!"

Maggie grinned, "So, they meet your approval?"

"Oh, wow, absolutely! But what's your date going to think when you were all, you know, pretty flat when he asked you out, and now you're all, well, you're all - oh my gawwd!"

"Would you quit saying oh my gawwd! Get used to my new look because this is the new me," Maggie said as she did a curtsy. "The new and improved Maggie McCoy! Oh, and Dave's never met me. Clint set us up, so it's all good."

"So, what are you going to do, you know, if he tries to cop a feel?" Laura asked with a sly grin on her face.

"Hey," Maggie replied, "I'm not that kind of girl!"

THE RED BRA

Laughing, Laura touted, "Well, you better be careful what you advertise if it's not for sale!"

Maggie picked Thumper up off the floor and threw it at Laura.

Ah, Laura thought, staring into the empty glass of wine. *I haven't thought about Maggie in forever. I wonder what's going on in her world now.*

Well, RB thought, *that whole water bra thing sounds kind of well, kind of ridiculous! OMG, I am so freaking glad my owner was well endowed and never resorted to bouncing around with water balloons over her titties! Can you imagine if one burst? Oh, too funny.*

Hmm, more wine, yes or no? Laura mused, running her finger along the rim of the glass. She glanced at the clock. It was only 8:00, and her shift at Walmart didn't begin until 10 AM the following morning. *One more glass, that's it, just one more glass,* she thought, walking back into the kitchen. Laura refilled her glass and walked down the hall to Riley's room. She stood silently at the door for a few seconds. She could hear Riley's music playing. Words about midnight memories were filling her room. *At least I can be thankful she doesn't listen to rap,* Laura thought as she tapped on the door and entered without waiting for a response. Riley was sitting at her desk with a textbook open. She picked up her pencil and wrote in her notebook without acknowledging her mother's intrusion.

"So," Laura said as she sat on the edge of the bed. "What are you working on?"

"Social studies."

"Oh, I was never good at social studies. Honestly, I wasn't much good at school work at all," Laura said, lifting the wine glass to her mouth.

Riley lifted her head and glanced over at her mother with a quizzical look and wondered what force brought her mother into her bedroom for a chat. Riley saw the wine glass and sighed. *Yeah, that was it, her mother turned into Chatty Cathy when she drank too much.*

"I'm kinda busy, Mom. This report is due tomorrow, and I really need to finish it."

"Shush, I want to hear the song you're playing," Laura said. Although it came out more as 'slush', Riley noted.

"I kinda like that," Laura said. "Who's the band?"

"One D, now Mom, can you please let me do my homework."

"Midnight memories, oh boy. Did I ever tell you about the time your dad and I were stumbling down the street and singing?"

Riley wasn't sure she wanted to hear that story. When her mom was drinking, she had a tendency to give TMI.

"Ma... I *really* need to finish my homework. Maybe lat—"

Laura cut her off.

"You know, I really did love your daddy," Laura said, raising the glass of wine to her lips. "He was smart and clever too! We had gone to one of the frat parties

Maggie's boyfriend belonged to. That was the first time I ever played beer pong, and well, you know my skills at ping pong. We got totally trashed," Laura said, falling back on the bed and sloshing wine on the comforter.

Riley had to bite her tongue to keep from commenting on the spilled wine. She had been subjected to her mother's wine-soaked ramblings too many times to count. She knew if she pretended to listen and said uh huh every now and then, her mother would eventually pass out and not remember sharing details of her life that no eleven-year-old daughter ever needed to know.

"Anyway, that night I was wearing my new water bra," Laura said as she leaned up on her elbow and took another swallow of wine.

The words 'water bra' caused Riley's ears to perk up, and she turned to face her mother with a modicum of interest.

Laura looked at Riley as she sat up and placed her wine glass on the bedside table. "A waater bra," Laura said, "ish a bra that has these pouches of water you put right chere." Laura lifted her shirt with her free hand and placed it on the lower portion of her bra.

Riley's face felt flush, and she turned her head, embarrassed for her mother.

"Wha, didn't you jus shay this evening that you wanted a bra?" "How can you exspect to wear a bra if you can't even look at your own mother's bra?" Laura's mother slurred, having exceeded her wine limit for the evening.

Being a little bit interested in finding out what this water bra thing was all about, Riley turned to her mother and smiled.

"Sure, Mom, tell me about it." Riley closed her textbook and turned her chair to face her mother.

"Well, Maggie showed me this water bra she had. Oh, my gawwd, did it make her titties look full," Laura said laughing. "Maggie was flatter than a pancake without that bra. I jus had to have one." Laura picked up her wine glass and took another sip. "Well, actually I gotch two. A black one and a beige one." Laura looked down at her breasts. "Shit, I should buy one now! Perk up these girls!" Laura picked up her wine glass and put it to her lips. Leaning her head back, she drained the rest of the glass before handing it to Riley. "Be a big girl and go fill up your mama's glass."

Riley took the glass and went to the kitchen as Laura flopped back down on the bed. She hated that her mom drank so much. Ever since her daddy left, Riley was aware her mom seemed to drink more and more. She opened the fridge and turned the spigot on the box of wine. She filled the glass almost to the brim. She had learned the hard way not to shortchange her mama on her glass of wine. Riley didn't mind filling her wine glass tonight because she thought maybe with all this water bra talk, maybe, just maybe, she could twist the conversation around to her getting a bra. *But not a water bra, eww,* Riley thought, wrinkling her nose.

THE RED BRA

Riley walked back into her bedroom. Laura lay sprawled on the bed, eyes closed, with Riley's iPod in her hand. "Midnight Memories" were spilling into the room. Riley coughed, and Laura opened her eyes.

"Oh, shank you schweetie," Laura slurred as she sat up and reached for her wine glass. "That song sho reminds me of the waater bra night."

Riley briefly wondered if it was really called a waater bra, with the a sound drug out, or if that was just the wine talking.

"Now, mind you," Laura said, "Daddy knew my girls normally weren't ash big ash they were that evening. I noticed him noticing them if you know what I mean," Laura said with a wobbly-headed wink. "So, like I was shayin, your daddy and I were walking home from the frat party, and I was scwearin my new waater bra. This was jush our third date, and well, we'd done a little touchy-feely, but..."

"Mom!" Riley exclaimed, "Really, I don't need to know all the details!"

"Well, little missy, you *will* need to learn these things, and who better to teach you than your mama! Now, where was I? Oh, yeah, Joel, I mean Daddy, was swalking me back to my dorm. We were arm in arm and singing at the top of our lungs! Hmm, what were we shinging, oh yeah, I remember, "Paradise by the Dashboard Lights"! You've heard that song, haven't you schweetie? Laura took a gulp of wine and started singing about forever love at the top of her lungs.

Riley leaned back in her chair and closed her eyes. *Oh, lordy, here we go. How long til the waterworks.*

The thought was barely complete when Laura's singing stopped as abruptly as it began. Her eyes welled up, the tears spilling out and running down her face.

"Ahhh, why did he leave me? God, tell me why?" Laura bawled as she looked up at the ceiling, her bloodshot eyes now raining tears as fast and sudden as a spring shower.

Riley got up and sat on the bed next to her mother. She put her arm around her, and Laura laid her head on Riley's shoulder.

"I'm shorry," she hiccupped. "Sometimes I jus mish him show much."

"I know, Mama, I do too," Riley said, taking the wine glass from her mother's hand.

"It's getting late, and I need to go to school tomorrow. Why don't you finish telling me about the water bra tomorrow?"

"Aghh," Laura wailed. "I want another waater bra! I want to be young and sexy feeling again."

Laura lifted her head from Riley's shoulder while turning her body to face Riley, her tears subsiding as fast as they began. "Riley," Laura began, her words still mixed with wine. "Maybe we should get you a braaa!" Her hand flopped down and landed on the lower edges of Riley's shirt. Her fingers clasped the bottom hem as she shifted her position and began to pull it up.

"Mom!" Riley yelled. Startled, she jumped up to get out of her mother's reach.

THE RED BRA

"What? For god's shake, I gave birth to you! I can look at chor buds if I want to!" Laura said indignantly.

Riley smoothed her shirt down and cast a wary glance at her mother.

"You never finished telling me what happened with the water bra," Riley said, attempting to keep her mother's paws off her budding flowers.

"Oh," Laura said with a wave of her hand, "long story short, they leaked."

Riley really didn't want to know how they happened to leak, but she did still want to continue talking about bras, so she sat back down next to her mother.

Oh, Riley, RB thought, *don't be such a party pooper! I want to know how they leaked! Did they explode and spray water all over Joel's face, or did they just dribble and make her look like a breastfeeding mama who was late for a feeding?* RB ceased her thoughts of bra-breast leakage when she heard Riley mention the word, 'bra.'

"Mom, Sydney has a bra."

"Well, she does, now does she?"

"Yeah, and so does Sophia, and I think Sara and Elizabeth have one too."

Laura leaned back and eyed Riley in the chest. "Then I guessh it's time you gotch one too," she said, standing up and wobbling towards the door. "I sthink I needth to go to bed. We'll talk mo tomorrow.

"Ok Mom, sleep tight."

"Huh," Riley said after her mother left the room, a grin beginning to spread across her face. "I'm going to get a bra!" she said excitedly. She grabbed her phone and texted Sydney.

Mom said I could get a bra!

OMG

Yeah, right, gotta go. Have to finish my SS report.

ttyl

K

Riley sat at her desk and opened her social studies book. She noticed the doggie pencil sitting nearby and picked it up.

"So, my little French poodle," she began in the best French accent she could muster. "I do not need you to get a bra, so ta ta," she giggled, tossing the pencil to the side.

Oh, I love that little girl, RB thought as she shimmied her cups. *Or rather I should say, young lady since she will soon be amongst the ranks of the bra-wearing population! What a peach! I'd like to smack that sot of a mama across her face and tell her to wake up and be thankful for her precious little darling.*

THE RED BRA

***

Riley arose to the sounds of birds chirping outside her window. Reaching over to the bedside table, she lifted her phone. 7:07 shone out above the photo of her, Julia and Sydney that they all used for the wallpaper on their phones. Riley lay her phone back down on the table, and her hand brushed against the wine glass her mother had left there the night before. The glass, more than half full, started to teeter. Riley quickly grabbed the glass and stilled its sloshing contents. She sat up, both hands now on the wine glass and gingerly set the glass back on the nightstand. *Wow, that was close,* she thought, using her thumb to wipe a small drop of wine that had splashed on the table. Riley wiped her thumb on her pajama bottoms then stood up and stretched her arms high above her head. She caught a glimpse of herself in the mirror, her pajama top rising and exposing the lower portion of her flat stomach. Riley lowered her arms and stood sideways to the mirror. Smoothing her pajama top tightly against her skin, she grinned at the lumps reflected in the mirror. *I have breasts! Mom said I could get a bra!* Riley grinned from ear to ear. She couldn't wait to get to school and talk to Sydney and Julia.

Cleo came strolling into Riley's bedroom. Her plaintive meow demanding food. Riley picked up Cleo and hugged her fiercely. "Oh, Cleo, I love you so much, and don't you worry, I promise I will keep your litter box clean, clean, clean, so Mama doesn't try to get rid of you." Riley walked to the laundry room holding Cleo close to her neck. She leaned down and buried her nose in the soft fur as she quietly passed her mother's bedroom. Laura's door was partway open, and Riley could hear her snuffling snores before she saw her. Still clothed, Laura was lying in bed with a sheet partially draped over her legs. Riley put a single finger to her lip in a 'shh' motion as Cleo looked up to Riley.

Riley fed Cleo and checked the litter box for 'sand castles'. She didn't want to risk getting her mother mad again and blow her chance of getting a bra. Going through her usual morning routine for a school day, she bathed, dressed, fixed herself a bowl of cereal, and sat alone at the kitchen table eating her Captain Crunch. Laura rarely got up before Riley left for school because she usually worked the ten to five shift and saw no sense in getting up before nine. Riley finished eating, put her bowl and spoon in the dishwasher, grabbed her backpack, and headed out the door. The school was only a few blocks away, and she smiled, resisting the urge to skip rather than walk. Julia rode the bus, and Sydney's older sister, Amanda, who was in high school, had a car and drove her to school. The girls always met around eight o' clock each morning near the flagpole so they could visit before the 8:25 bell rang, and they had to begin their school day.

When Riley arrived at the flagpole, Sydney was already there. Riley ran up behind Sydney and laid her hands on her shoulders and jumped in the air. Riley was grinning like a Cheshire cat as Sydney turned around, smiling back at her. They grasped hands and jumped up and down laughing.

"Your mom said you could get a b-"

"Sh," Riley dropped one of Sydney's hands and put her finger to her lips before Sydney could finish. "We can't talk here," she said, turning her head and nodding to the group of students milling around the flagpole. Still clasping one of Sydney's hands, Riley dragged her friend past the flagpole and down the sidewalk to the corner of the school building where no students were standing.

"Well, come on, tell me," Sydney said, her excitement for her friend showing in her voice.

"Mom was, um, let's say she was, uh, thirsty last night, and she came into my room to, I don't know, hang out I guess. You know, since Dad's not there anymore I think sometimes she gets a little lonely. Anyway, she was telling me this story about when she and Dad were dating, and she began talking about a water bra her college roommate had, and well, I don't know, she said I could get a bra!"

"Wait a minute," Sydney said, holding her hand up in the air by Riley's face. "What's a water bra?"

Riley rolled her eyes, "Don't even ask, all I know is she said I could get a bra! Where did you get yours? How did you know what size to get? Did you have to try it on in the store?" Riley could hardly contain her excitement as she jumped up and down, realizing she wanted a bra more than she thought. "Sydneyeeee," Riley said almost breathless, "do you think I can come over to your house after school and you can, you know, show me your bras?" In her heightened state, she didn't see Julia approaching.

"Uh, hi guys," Julia said as she neared her friends. "You sure look happy today Riley, did you get a toy in your cereal box this morning?"

"Ha, funny," Riley retorted. "You will never guess what my mom agreed to!"

"She can get a bra!" Sydney interrupted, a little too loudly for Riley's comfort.

"Shhh, I don't want the whole world to know," Riley admonished her friend.

"Reeaallly?" Julia dragged the word out while cocking her head sideways and squinting her eyes while staring at Riley.

"Yeah, now you need to ask your mom for one, and we can go shopping together!" Riley replied oblivious to Julia's squinty-eyed stare.

"I need to go in and talk to Mrs. Stewart about one of the math problems from last night's homework," Julia replied. "I'll catch you later." Julia quickly turned and headed for the door.

"Wait a minute," Riley yelled to her friend. Julia pretended not to hear and entered the building. Turning to face Sydney, Riley said, "What's wrong with her? She blew me off last night when I texted her too."

"I don't know. Maybe she thinks her mom won't let her get a bra."

"Yeah, well, her mom's always been kinda cool. I get the feeling Julia doesn't want one."

"Hey, I know," Sydney said. "Why don't I ask my mom if you and Julia can spend the night tonight. We can try on my bras and that way Julia can see they're not so bad."

"Sounds like a plan," Riley said, lifting her hand to give Sydney a high five.

The bell rang, and the girls walked to the entrance. Happy it was Friday, they walked down the hall to their lockers and gathered their books before heading to their first-hour class. This was their first year having lockers and changing classrooms for different subjects. The girls felt grown-up using the lockers and sitting in desks like they had in the high school.

During lunch, the girls plopped down at their usual table. Sydney sat next to Riley and Julia sat across from them. Sophia was a few seats down, along with Alicia, Scott, and James. Scott and James lived in the same neighborhood as Sydney and had enjoyed many kickball games in Sydney's spacious backyard.

"Hey," Sydney said to Julia in between bites of the sloppy joe the lunch ladies had prepared. "You wanna spend the night at my house tonight? Riley's gonna come too. I still need to ask my mom, but I'm pretty sure it will be okay, you know she loooves my besties!"

"Um," Julia began as she picked at the tater tots on her tray.

"Sure she does," Riley quipped, "it will be fun! What else ya gonna do?"

"I don't know, I – hey," she yelled as Scott reached over with his fork and stabbed one of her tater tots and shoved it into his mouth.

"Well, you weren't eatin' them," Scott teased. "Can't waste food you know, all those starving kids in China and all."

Julia grinned, and Riley cast a dirty look at Scott.

"Okay, it's set. We're having a sleepover, right Julia?" Riley said, picking up her milk carton and taking a long drink.

"Yeah, I guess," Julia replied. "Sydney, text me after you ask your mom."

"Yeah, me too," Riley said, now grinning as she anticipated an evening of trying on bras.

Sophia raised her body and leaned over the table. Facing Sydney, she shouted, "Hey, you having a sleepover? I know my mom will let me come. I got *Despicable Me 2* on blue ray. You do have a blue-ray player, don't you? I could bring it. Oh, and I could bring some of my new outfits, and we could combine our wardrobes, and we could..."

Riley looked across the table at Julia and rolled her eyes. Julia giggled as Sydney tried to interrupt Sophia.

"Uh, Sophia," Sydney began, trying to cut off Sophia's incessant yammering.

"... paint our nails, and oh, I have an Ouija board, you know what that is, don't you?" Sophia continued, oblivious to Sydney's attempts to say something.

"Sophia!" Riley shouted hoping to be heard above the din of seventy-two fifth graders all seemingly talking at once.

Everyone at their table and it seemed all the tables around them stopped talking and stared at Riley. "Geez," Riley said, "do you ever stop talking? Sydney is *trying* to say something to you." Alicia let out a laugh that was more of a snort. James poked her and called her a pig while Scott took the opportunity to snitch another tater tot from Julia's tray. The other students quickly lost interest and turned back to their own tables' commotions.

"What?" Sophia said a bit indignantly, "I bet *you* don't have Despicable Me 2 on blue ray!"

"Sophia, you don't invite yourself to other people's sleepovers," Riley said between clenched teeth. The last thing Riley needed was the Queen of Bradom coming over and showing off her two-thousand bras of every color under the sun.

Sophia glanced at Sydney then turned back to face Riley and glared. "Well," she huffed, "I don't believe YOU are the one having the sleepover." She turned her head back to Sydney and quickly changed her glare to a sweet smile. Riley noticed Sophia had a chunk of sloppy joe bun with a bit of meat stuck to her front brace, and she smiled.

"Um, sorry Sophia," Sydney said meekly, "but my mom only lets me have two girls over at a time, and I already asked Riley and Julia."

Sophia flopped back down in her seat. "I didn't want to come over anyway. Besides, I'm having a HUGE sleepover in a couple of weeks, and my mom lets me have as many girls over as I want."

"Yeah, right," Riley said under her breath while intercepting Scott's fork as he dove in for another of Julia's tater tots. Scott's fork flew across the table and landed with a clatter on the floor at the feet of the lunchroom monitor. "Oh, crap," Riley whispered as she and everyone else at the table suddenly became serious about eating their food.

"So," the monitor began, "anyone missing a fork?"

Alicia started to speak, but just as the words were coming out of her mouth, Scott kicked her beneath the table. Alicia squealed, and the monitor's dark brown eyes focused on her.

"Is this your fork, Alicia?"

"Nope, got mine right here," she said as she waved it in the air, tossing bits of sloppy joe about the table.

"Oh, gross, Alicia, you are so gross," James said as Alicia continued to wave her fork around a little more violently, causing the remaining sauce to slide off and land on the edge of Scott's tray.

"I'm outta here," Scott said, standing and picking up his tray, careful not to touch Alicia's sauce that was dripping off the edge.

"Mrs. Swanson," Scott said to the monitor, "I'll take that fork back with my tray if you would like."

"Why thank you, Scott," she said with a smile before facing the table and sternly admonishing the group to learn some manners.

Once Mrs. Swanson was out of earshot, the table cracked up with waves of laughter. "That Scott is one smooth dude," Julia said. "I think I'll go buy him some tater tots."

Hmmm, RB thought wistfully, *I think Julia may like that Scott boy. I must say, he is pretty smooth for an eleven-year-old! But, oh! More importantly, a sleepover! How exciting!* RB exclaimed. *Oooh, I can't wait to watch my budding, young flowers take the first steps towards being ladies! What fun this will be! Too bad Sophia can't come. I would love to take a peek at that scarlet bra*

Chapter 4
Sydney and Julia

"Ma, I'm home," Sydney hollered, dropping her backpack on the dining room table, half skipping, half walking into the kitchen, the smell of fresh baked cookies permeating the air.

Sydney walked into the kitchen and snitched a warm oatmeal cookie from the cooling rack on the counter. "Yum," she said between bites as bits of cookie scattered down her shirt. "These are good!"

"Sydney," her mother, Sarah, admonished, "where are your manners? Say hello to Annabelle."

"Oh, gosh, I didn't see you," Sydney said, looking up from the cookies while wiping crumbs from her shirt. Julia's mother was sitting at the counter sipping a cup of hot tea, the steam rising, its herbal scent mingling with the aroma of cookies filling the air with deliciousness.

Sarah was a stay at home mom and was grateful she could be home to greet her children when they returned home from school each day. She loved to cook and was proud of the garden she planted each spring, complete with an herb bed.

"No worries," Annabelle responded with a smile. "Those cookies would distract anyone! Quite the baker your mother is. And what about this tea! Your mother tells me you helped mix the herbs to create all these wonderful flavors."

"Yeah," Sydney responded, "Have you tried the one with sage and lemon thyme? That's my fav."

"Not yet, but I'll be sure to try it." Annabelle smiled as she responded to Sydney.

"Um," Sydney said, turning to her mother. "I was wondering if Riley and Julia could spend the night tonight."

"Sure, hon, that's fine with me." She turned to Annabelle. "Is that okay with you?"

"Yeah, truthfully it would be great. There's a movie Jon and I want to see. This will give us the chance to have a date night."

Sydney wrinkled her nose. "Married people have date nights?"

"Well of course, silly, just because we're married doesn't mean we don't still like a little romance!"

"Um, okay," Sydney replied, not sure what to think about parents having dates.

"How's Riley doing these days?" Annabelle asked. "She hasn't been to the house in a while. Julia said she spends every other weekend with her dad. I would imagine the divorce has been hard on her."

"Yeah, well, I don't know, she doesn't talk about it much, but oh, Mom," Sydney's eyes lit up as she faced her mother, "Riley's mom said she could get a bra!" As soon

43

as the words left her lips, Sydney clasped her hand over her mouth. She looked back and forth from her mother to Annabelle. *"Pleeease* don't tell Riley I said that!"

The ladies smiled. "It's ok," Annabelle said. "Your secret is safe with us. Actually, just last week I mentioned going bra shopping to Julia."

Sydney's eyes opened wide. "You did?"

Annabelle chuckled lightly, "Now you need to keep *my* secret, and not tell Julia I told you as I'm guessing from your reaction she didn't tell you."

"No way! You told her she could get a bra! Whenever Riley and I start talking about bras she gets all weird on us. We thought maybe you wouldn't let her have one."

Annabelle wrinkled her brow.

"Oh gosh, sorry. Riley said you were way cool and you would probably let her get one." Sydney quickly added, "I think you're cool too, we just, well, we couldn't figure out why she, you know, kinda avoided the whole bra talk."

Annabelle smiled at Sydney. "No worries, my dear. Julia is, how should I say this, a little confused about her changing body. Well, maybe not confused, but shy. She has always been modest. Gosh, back in the potty training days she would close the door on me and say, *I do it myself.*" Annabelle smiled at the memory. "Wow," she turned to Sarah, when did our girls grow up?"

"The time has sure flown by," Sarah said, walking around the counter and putting her arm around Sydney.

"Oh, Mom," Sydney said, wiggling out from beneath her mother's tightening embrace. "I need to text Riley so she can ask her mom if she can come over. What time can they come?"

"If you girls are up for burgers, they can come over anytime. I bet I can talk your dad into firing up the grill. I'd like to take advantage of the last of these beautiful fall evenings. Annabelle, you and Jon can join us if you'd like.

"Oh, thanks, Sarah, but I'm hoping Jon and I can go out to dinner before the movie."

"Understood," Sarah said with a wink.

"Speaking of Jon, I better scoot on home. He should be home soon. How about if I drop Julia off on our way out, probably, oh I don't know, in an hour or so?"

"Sounds great, okay with you Sydney?"

"Um, yeah," Sydney said, pulling her phone out of her back pocket and heading to her room to text Riley. "See you later, Annabelle."

Mom said yes to a sleepover

She eyed the disarray and began scooping up clothes as she waited for Riley to respond to her text. She tossed clothes into the laundry basket in her closet and used her foot to push shoes, notebooks, and hair bands under the bed. "Good enough," Sydney said out loud as she walked to her dresser to make sure she still had a couple of bras in her drawer.

Interesting, RB mused. *I wonder what's up with Julia not wanting a bra. Perhaps I should check on my little, confused flower.* RB tightened her straps while lifting her

45

DD's in the fall breeze and sailing through the afternoon sky. She followed the winding country roads arriving at Julia's home just as Julia was stepping off the bus.

Julia hopped off the bus and trotted down the lane. "Ma," she hollered as she entered the house, dropping her backpack on the floor near the entryway. She walked into the kitchen and saw the note on the fridge.

I'm at Sarah's XOXO Mom.

Julia opened the fridge and hung on the door while staring at its contents. Finding nothing to suit her mood, she closed the door and began opening cabinets. "Cereal, nope; fig newtons, nope; pretzel sticks nope." Julia returned to the refrigerator and opened the door again. She moved the milk carton, shuffled the yogurt, and peeked behind the left-over spaghetti, still finding nothing that made her taste buds tingle. She walked back to the cabinet that housed the pretzel sticks and grabbed a couple. Julia sat at the breakfast bar in the kitchen and slowly began licking the salt chunks off her pretzel. As the pretzel stick became gooey, she nibbled on the outer coating. Julia paused and looked at her pretzel.

Kinda looks like a pencil, she thought. *I could invent a new edible pencil.* Giggling she held it between her fingers like a pencil and pretended to draw a heart in the air. *Penzel, that's what I'll call my new invention! I'll become rich and famous, and Penzel stores will be all over the world!* Julia smiled and began to spin herself around on the bar stool. Midway through her spin, her mind flew back to pencils, and the elusive pencil test. "What ev," she muttered, lowering the pretzel and biting off a huge chunk. Chomping on her now salt-less pretzel she began to think about the pencil test, and for the life of her she could not figure out what the heck it could have to do with needing a bra. She spun her stool around and noticed her mother's laptop sitting on the counter. *Hmm,* she thought, reaching over and pulling the computer in front of her. She got up and looked out the window to make sure her mother wasn't pulling in the drive. She raced back to the kitchen and googled 'pencil test'. Urban Dictionary popped up, and she clicked on the link.

The Pencil Test is a test to determine if a woman needs a bra or not. If the woman can hold a pencil under her breast without dropping it, then they pass the test and therefore need a bra.

Oh, Julia thought, licking the salt off her second pretzel. *That's weird.*

As Julia considered how a pencil could possibly stick under Sophia's boobs, she heard the garage door open. Quickly she closed the computer and scooted it back where it was and hopped off the bar stool to greet her mother.

"Hi Hon," Annabelle said as she entered the kitchen, dropping her purse on the counter and smiling at her daughter. "How was school today?"

"Oh, ya know, same ol' stuff."

"Was Mrs. Stuart able to help you with your math before school?"

"Yeah, I think I get it now."

"That's great," Annabelle said as she walked over to her laptop and opened the lid.

Oh crap, Julia thought, *did I close Urban Dictionary?*

Before she could finish her thought, the look on her mother's face told her she hadn't.

"Hmm, what's this?" Annabelle said, turning the computer screen to face Julia.

Julia's cheeks instantly turned bright red, and she lowered her eyes without responding.

Annabelle walked around the counter and gently put her hand on Julia's chin, lifting her face and looking into her brown eyes, now brimming with tears.

"Oh, honey," Annabelle crooned, taking Julia into her arms. No longer able to hold back the tears, Julia succumbed to her mother's loving embrace as the tears flowed freely down her face. "Baby, it's ok. Talk to mama, what's going on in that pretty little head of yours?"

Julia shook her head and buried her face deeper into the crook of her mother's neck.

Annabelle hugged her daughter tightly, wishing she could somehow make the angst of the pre-teen years magically disappear.

"It's just that," Julia began while squeezing her eyes shut in an attempt to stop the flow of tears before she continued to speak. Taking a deep breath and inhaling the scent of her mother, the words began to rush out. "Sophia has all these bras, and she's always making fun of me and Riley for not having one, and she said Riley couldn't even

48

pass a pencil test, and well…" Taking another deep breath before continuing she quietly said, "I didn't know what she meant so I looked it up. You're not mad, are you?"

"Mad? Oh sweetie, of course not, why would I be mad at you?"

"I don't know," Julia snuffled before breaking away from her mother's embrace and wiping the tears from her eyes.

"It's just well, today Riley said her mom told her she could get a bra, and Sydney already has one, and…" Julia's cheeks began to burn as she felt the tell-tale signs of them beginning to redden while the tears once again overtook her and began to spill down her cheeks. Hanging her head, she watched a tear-drop as it found its way to the floor, silently landing on the tile beside her Nike-clad feet.

Annabelle put her hand on Julia's shoulder. "Honey, don't you remember last week when I asked you if you wanted to get a bra?"

"You don't understand!" Julia said, pulling away from her mother, the tears now flowing in a steady stream.

"Then talk to me, sweetie."

"I, uh, uh," Julia tried to speak as her sobs turned her words into hiccups and fell incoherently out of her mouth. Spinning on her heel, she turned and ran into her bedroom. Flinging herself face down on her bed, she sobbed.

Annabelle paused for a moment, unsure of what had just transpired. She knew the tweens were a difficult time, and her heart ached for her only daughter. Quietly, she walked down the hall towards Julia's room. Silently standing at the door she watched Julia's body heave up and down, her sobs muffled by Fluffy, the stuffed dog she received for her seventh birthday, pressed close to her face. How she ached for her daughter as she watched the tears push out the sadness and uncertainty that comes with growing up.

Annabelle silently turned and walked back to the kitchen. She understood Julia's need to be alone to sort out her feelings. They would talk later. She was glad her daughter was going to be with Riley and Sydney for the night. Perhaps she would open up to her friends.

Oh, the poor girl, RB threw her straps inward, processing the scene which had just played out before her. *What could possibly be preventing her from wanting a bra? Good grief, someone needs to explain to her how wonderful and supportive we are! How we create smooth lines on your attire, how we prevent jiggles and hide cold nipples! Well, she is still just a young thing, and I guess I can see how having ta-tas suddenly appear could make a young lady fearful.*

Julia knew her mother had been standing in her doorway and was relieved when she left without coming in. She rolled over and held Fluffy close to her chest. She was so confused. Part of her wanted to get a bra. She wanted to fit in with the other girls, but the truth was, she didn't want anyone to see her breasts, and she didn't know how she could manage to go about getting a bra without her mother seeing her bare breasts. She knew if she had a bra Riley and Sydney would want to see it too. "Oh Fluffy," she softly said, burying her face in his ratty time-worn cotton fur. "It's just not fair. Why can't my breasts be the same size! I bet Sophia's boobs aren't lopsided. What am I supposed to do?" she whispered in Fluffy's floppy ear. "Get two different sized bras and cut 'em up and sew 'em together!" *Yeah, like that would work,* she wryly thought, *seeing as I can't even thread a needle.*

RB swiftly threw her straps back and just as quickly tossed them straight up in the air. *OMG! Did I really hear that? Cut up a lovely bra! Wait a minute... Julia's buds are different sizes! No wonder she's been acting so odd!*

Julia sat up and threw her legs over the side of her bed. Grabbing a tissue from the bedside table, she wiped her tears off Fluffy's fur before blowing her nose. She stood and walked over to her mirror and leaned in to look at her red-rimmed eyes, carefully avoiding looking down at her chest. She pulled the rubber band off her ponytail, brushed her hair, and began re-doing her ponytail when her mother once again appeared at her door.

"You ok?" Annabelle asked, slowly entering the room.

"Yeah, I don't know why I cry so easily anymore. I'm sorry, Mom." Julia said, grabbing hold of her mother's index finger the way she did as a toddler. They walked together to the kitchen.

"Let me fix you some hot cocoa." Annabelle smiled, and Julia released her hold on her mother's finger and sat down at the counter. Annabelle reached into the cabinet and picked up the cocoa. "You know, Julia, all these emotions you're feeling are because your body is changing, honey, and not only on the outside but on the inside as well. We women are full of crazy hormones." Annabelle paused and laughed. "Just ask your father! Why, when I was pregnant with you, I would even cry over commercials! It's okay, you're normal."

Hearing the words 'you're normal', Julia began to tear up. She put the heels of her hands on her eyes, willing the waterfall that was teetering on the brim of her lower lids to stop before they flowed over her lashes and down her cheeks.

"No, I'm not, Mom, I'm not normal!" Julia blurted out as her lashes, unable to hold back the flood, unleashed a swell of tears that flowed in a steady stream down her face.

"Oh, baby, please, talk to me," Annabelle said, placing the cocoa on the counter and reaching out to embrace her only child.

Julia pulled back from her touch. Annabelle winced. A lump rose in her throat, and she tried not to let her face belie the pain her heart was enduring. Annabelle knew this day was coming. She remembered her youth, and the times she had rejected her mother.

Seeing the hurt in her mother's eyes, Julia reached out and grasped her mother's hand. "I'm sorry, Mom, really, I am." The words came out slowly, choked by tears and hiccups of breath.

"Then talk to me, baby, please, there's nothing we can't work out together."

Taking a deep breath, Julia looked up at her mother. Wiping her eyes, she looked down at the floor and quietly mumbled, "My breasts aren't the same size."

Annabelle cocked her head; not certain what Julia had said. "What about your breasts?" she gently asked.

"I knew you wouldn't understand!" Julia said looking up at her mother, unexpected anger rising within her and showing in her voice.

"No, I just couldn't hear you, that's all."

"Well, I'm a freak, okay!" Julia said, anger now taking over her emotions. The tears stopped their incessant flowing as Julia clenched her fists at her side. "MY TITTIES ARE TWO DIFFERENT SIZES!" she shouted. "CAN YOU HEAR ME NOW?"

Annabelle's mouth dropped open. Aghast that her soft-spoken child would yell at her; her mind froze for an instant. She closed her mouth, and before she could think of a response to the delicate situation, Julia turned and ran back to her bedroom and slammed the door. She stood still at the foot of her bed for several minutes, her fists still clenched at her sides and her breath coming out in heavy gasps. Fluffy, with his crooked tail and worn coat, stared at her from the bed; his glassy eyes looking on accusingly.

"What are you staring at?" she said, reaching over and roughly picking him up from the bed. She tightened her hands around his neck and choked her stuffed childhood friend with all her strength. "Stuffed animals are for babies, and I'm not a baby anymore." She tossed her once beloved toy to the corner and threw herself on the bed.

Oh crap! RB fiercely shook herself, *I know having always been with grown-up girls I've never experienced the growing stages, but surely this is temporary, and they will even out eventually!*

Annabelle stood still in the kitchen, the hot cocoa preparation forgotten. A single tear rolled down her cheek as she tried to wrap her head around what had just happened.

"Hon," Jon said, walking into the kitchen.

Annabelle jumped, so deep in thought, she had not heard him come in.

Jon walked over to the stove and turned off the whistling kettle.

"Didn't you hear the kettle?" Jon asked, turning to face Annabelle. Pausing for a moment, he looked intently at his wife. Noticing the tear-streaked stain on her face, he walked over to her and put his hands on either side of her face and looked into her red-rimmed brown eyes.

"What's going on?" he softly asked.

"Oh, Jon," Annabelle responded, wrapping her arms around his waist she tried to pull him close.

Jon slid his hands from Annabelle's face down to her waist and leaned back, forcing her to look up at him.

"Is everything ok? Where's Julia?" Jon asked with growing concern.

"Yes, no, I don't know," Annabelle said, releasing her hold on Jon and sitting down on the bar stool.

"Julia and I had a, well, not really a fight, but well, I guess her hormones are starting to kick in, and, oh Jon, she yelled at me!"

"She did what?" Jon asked, astonished that his mild-mannered daughter could have possibly yelled at her mother.

"I was…" Annabelle pointed to the steaming kettle on the stove, "fixing her some hot cocoa. She was, well, is, having a tough time dealing with, uh, female issues."

"Oh," Jon said, a slight smile appearing on his face, happy it wasn't anything serious.

"Now, Jon, don't take this lightly!" Annabelle admonished her husband.

Jon tried to look stern to appease his wife. Having three older sisters, two of whom were twins, he had been exposed to many bouts of crying and shouting between the girls and their mother, and between the girls themselves. He remembered when he was eight years old, and he went to his father during one particularly feisty shouting, crying, pouting match that was going on between the twins and their mother. His father was sitting in the recliner reading the evening paper totally oblivious to all the commotion going on in the dining room. Jon walked in and sat on the arm of his chair. His father lowered the Wall Street Journal and looked at him over his bifocals. "Women, Son, they're just women. Get used to it. In a few minutes they'll be hugging and kissing, and they won't even remember they were fussing." His father winked. "A word of advice, when you're grown and married, there are two words you must remember, and that's simply, 'yes, dear.' Now scoot," his father said as he rattled his paper and resumed reading.

"Yes, dear," Jon responded to Annabelle's admonishment, trying to keep the smile out of his voice as he remembered his father's sage advice. *Pop would be proud.*

"Jon!" Annabelle retorted, "Seriously, I'm worried about her."

"Did she, uh," Jon lowered his voice to a whisper, "start her, uh, her monthly thing?"

"What? Lord, no, but I expect it won't be long before that happens. No, it's," she paused, unsure how much to tell her husband as she knew Julia would be mortified if she knew she had spoken to her father about her breasts. Annabelle got up from the bar stool. She put her palm up in the air facing Jon, "Hang on a second." She quietly walked down the hall and made sure Julia's door was still closed. Annabelle tiptoed back into the kitchen.

Jon grinned at her, "What's with the Ninja moves?" he inquired.

"Oh hush," Annabelle said, lightly swatting Jon on the arm. "It's time for Julia to get a bra," she whispered.

Jon threw his head back and began laughing but quickly regained his composure when he saw *that* look on

Annabelle's face. Straightening the smile from his lips, he pulled her close, nuzzling his lips by her ear, he whispered, "Yes, dear."

Holy Moly! RB said, trying to understand the things she had heard. *I guess now I get why she doesn't want to talk to the girls about bras, and I'm glad Annabelle didn't tell Jon, but I sure hope she figures out a way to talk to Julia about this! Wow, I guess I better go check on my bud, Riley. I hope her mother's sober!*

Chapter 5
Sleep-over

Riley was sitting Indian style on her bed. Cleo was curled up in a ball and resting comfortably in the triangle created by her legs. Riley shifted, and Cleo lifted her head and yawned before stretching her front legs, exposing her claws and lightly digging them into Riley's calf at the same moment her phone whooshed. "Ahh!" Riley yelled as she jumped, startled by both the phone's sound breaking the silence in her room as well as by her cat's claws. Riley removed Cleo's claws from the denim of her jeans and gently lifted her and plopped her on the bed beside her. "You goofy cat," she said, giving Cleo a pat on the head while sliding off the bed, "That hurt!" Cleo turned her head towards Riley, her eyes mere slits with the green irises barely showing around her diamond shaped pupils. She lay her head down, closed her eyes completely, and stretched while once more baring her claws as if to say, *watch it, honey; there's more where that came from.*

Riley walked to her dresser and picked up her phone and read the text from Sydney.

Mom said yes to a sleep-over

Sweet! M not home should b soon

K, M said u can eat with us

K ttyl

Riley checked the time on her phone. *4:48, Mom should be home soon,* she thought, walking to the laundry room to make sure the litter box was spotless. *I don't want to give mom any reason to say no.* After cleaning out the litter box, she walked to the living room and turned on the TV. She had already carefully washed and dried her mother's wine glass and cleaned up the remnants of toast that lay scattered across the kitchen counter. Riley picked up the remote and began flipping through the channels when she noticed her mother's coffee cup on the end table. Dropping the remote on the couch, she picked up the lipstick stained cup and took it to the kitchen and placed it in the dishwasher. *That's a good sign,* Riley thought. *At least Mom got up early enough to eat and drink her coffee before work. I sure hope she's in a good mood when she gets home. Surely a clean house will get a yes to letting me spend the night with Sydney.* Walking back to the living room, Riley heard her mother pull up in the driveway. Grabbing the remote, she clicked off the TV and ran to the door to greet her mother.

"Hi!" Riley said with a big smile on her face as she opened the door.

Furrowing her brow, she looked at Riley and said, "Ok, what do you want?"

Riley's grin spread as she stepped to the side to let her mother enter the house.

"Why do you think I want something? Can't I be happy to have my mama home?"

"I know you, kiddo," Laura said, tossing her purse on the coffee table and flopping on the couch. She lifted her feet and propped them on the coffee table, scooting her purse out of the way with her left loafer.

Cleo, rested from her most recent nap, strolled into the room and jumped on Laura's lap.

"Scoot!" Laura said, pushing her off the couch. "I don't need cat hair all over me." Cleo landed on the floor with a gentle thud. She sat back on her haunches and began licking her front leg, glancing up at Laura between licks as if to say, *you don't faze me, lady.*

Ooh, feisty cat, RB thought, watching her groom herself without taking her eyes off Laura. *You don't like her much, do you? I don't either.* Cleo stopped grooming and twitched her ears. *Well, all I can say is she better let Riley go to Sydney's. That girl needs some fun!*

Laura glanced from the cat to Riley and arched her eyebrow.

"Yes, Mom, Cleo's litter box is clean."

"That's my girl. God, my puppies hurt," she said, using her heel to slip off each loafer. One fell to the floor startling Cleo and causing her to dash out of the room.

Riley sat in the recliner and drummed her fingers on the arm of the chair.

"So, what's up?" Laura dryly inquired, her head thrown back on the couch with her eyes barely open.

"Um, Sydney asked me to spend the night. She said I could have supper with them too. Can I? Pleeease,"

Laura raised her head and opened her eyes. "You sure the litter box is clean? Dishes done? Room picked up?"

"Yup," Riley said, jumping off the chair and getting on her knees, her hands folded together in a praying position. She looked up to her mother imploring, "pleeeeease!"

"You goof, get up," Laura said, trying to hide a smile. "Sure, why not, some of the girls from work are getting together at the *Bee Hive* this evening. Perhaps I'll join them."

"Thank you, thank you, thank you so much, Mama," Riley said, jumping up from her knees to her feet in one swift move. She ran to the couch and leaned over and hugged her mother.

"Shoo," Laura said, pushing Riley away. "I need to rest if I'm going out tonight. Do you think Annabelle can you pick you up?"

"Yeah, sure," Riley said before skipping to her room to text Sydney.

I can stay over! Riley texted.

***

Sydney had just finished straightening up the drawer which housed her bras. It held two sport bras, one pink with light blue ribbing along the edges and one gray. Proceeding to her closet, she began rooting through her dirty laundry basket in search of more bras when her phone dinged. She read the text and did a short hop in the air before responding.

yeah!!! when can u come, Sydney responded.

Now if ur mom or Amanda pick me up

I'll check brb

"Ma," Sydney hollered while walking to the kitchen in search of her mother.

"Oh, hi Dad," Sydney said as she entered the kitchen where her father, Kyle, and her mom were seated at the breakfast bar. "I didn't know you were home," she said, reaching for an oatmeal cookie.

"Ah, ah," Sarah said, making a shooing motion with her hand over the cookies. "Save room for supper. Dad said he'd grill. How many of his super-duper burgers should he fix? Can Riley come?"

Sydney made a pouty face at her mother, chagrined at being denied a cookie, but she quickly turned her pout into a smile before saying, "Yeah, she just texted, but she needs a ride. Do you think you or dad could pick her up?"

Sarah glanced at the clock. "Your sister should be finishing up basketball practice. Why don't you text her and see if she can pick her up on the way home?"

"K," Sydney said, pulling her phone from her back pocket and texting Amanda.

plz pick up Riley on ur way home

Amanda, walking across the school parking lot and heading for her car looked at her phone. *Geez,* she thought begrudgingly, not *only am I Sydney's personal chauffeur, but she also expects me to chauffeur her friends!* She briefly considered ignoring the text but instead responded.

K

TY

Sydney quickly texted to her sister before sending Riley a text to confirm. Placing her phone on the counter, she stood behind her father and draped her arms over his shoulders.

Kyle grasped her right hand and turned his head to smile at his youngest daughter. "I guess this means I'm going to be surrounded by females this evening," he said with a slight chortle in his voice. "I think I hear the garage calling my name."

"Oh, Daddy," Sydney giggled, as he turned and tickled her side.

"I'll let you escape to your man cave after dinner," Sarah said, needing to speak loudly to be heard over the gigglefest which was now in full force since Sydney had fallen to the floor. Kyle bent over and tickled her on the side, delighted he could still elicit such uninhibited laughter from his daughter.

Kyle, bearing a wide smile, stood up and reached his hand out to Sydney and helped her to her feet. "What do you think?" he asked, "Twelve burgers? Two a piece?"

Sydney giggled. "We're girls, Daddy, one each is fine."

"Okay, but don't try sneaking bites out of my burger when yours is all gone." He winked at his wife. "Guess I better go fire up the grill."

Yeah! Sounds like the sleepover is going to happen! RB shimmied her straps with excitement. *I can't wait to see my young buds accept that they are growing up! But, oh, I sure hope Julia still gets to go!*

***

Riley grabbed her backpack from the floor by her bed where she had dropped it when she got home from school. She unzipped it and dumped the contents on her bed before going to her dresser and pulling out clean clothes to take to Sydney's. She shoved her clothes in the backpack and ran to the bathroom and grabbed her toothbrush and comb and shoved them in the pencil holder section of her backpack. She stood still, tapping her chin with her index finger thinking about what else she should bring. Looking at the books, papers, and pens scattered all over her bed, she walked over and using her arm as a shovel she pushed the clutter under her bedspread. Standing, she surveyed her bed and leaned over to ruffle the bedspread in an attempt to hide the mayhem. *Don't need mom getting mad about my messy room,* she thought as she grabbed her bag and headed to the living room. She entered the room just as Amanda pulled into the drive. She looked over at her mother, still in the same position on the couch, but with her eyes completely closed. Riley stopped, unsure whether to wake her to tell her she was leaving.

"I'm awake," Laura mumbled. Her eyes still closed, she raised her hand partway up before letting it fall limply on the couch.

"Amanda's here," Riley said in a voice not much higher than a whisper. "See you tomorrow, Mom." She quickly left the house and ran down the walkway and hopped in Amanda's car, fearful if she didn't leave fast enough her mom would change her mind.

***

Julia sat up in her bed, shame beginning to creep into her soul for the way she was behaving. *I don't know what's wrong with me,* she thought as she picked at the little balls of pilling on her blanket. *I probably blew my chance at spending the night with Sydney.* She continued to mindlessly pick at the little cotton balls, pulling them off and flicking them in the air. *Oh, well, I might as well go say I'm sorry and beg for forgiveness,* she said to herself before tossing her legs over the side of the bed and standing.

Quietly, Julia walked into the kitchen. Her mom and dad were sitting at the counter. Her dad turned in his chair, a big grin spread across his face. "Hi, Schnookums."

Julia couldn't help but smile when he called her by her pet name.

"You ready for some hot cocoa? I think the water's still warm," Annabelle asked.

"I'll take a cup if you're buying," Jon said, the smile still lighting up his face.

"Um, sure," Julia said while thinking, *Where are my parents, and who are these pod people?*

"So," Annabelle began, taking three mugs from the cabinet, "Sarah told me Sydney invited you to a sleepover tonight."

"Yeah," Julia said slowly beginning to wonder if she was going crazy and had just imagined that just a short while ago she had screamed at her mother.

"She said something to Riley and me during school, but she hadn't asked her mom yet."

"Sydney came home while I was there and asked Sarah. She said it was fine. She also said you could eat dinner with them. I think Kyle was going to grill burgers or something. It's fine with us if you'd like to go," her mother said as she spooned heaping tablespoons of cocoa into their mugs. "Marshmallows?" Her mother looked at her and smiled.

"Sure," Julia said, squinting at her mother, trying to decide if it really was her.

"Well, then, it's settled." Her mother began pouring tepid water and plopping marshmallows into the mugs. "I think your father and I will go to the new steakhouse in town and catch a movie. It's a win-win situation, don't you think?"

Jon raised his eyebrows and tilted his head while glancing over at Annabelle. *First I heard of dinner and a movie,* he thought to himself, *but hey, like she said, it's a win-win.* He grinned. *Ol' Pop was right, just give the ladies a few minutes, and their fussing and tears will turn into laughter. Or at least peace.*

Annabelle set the mugs of cocoa in front of Julia and Jon. Gripping the mug with both hands, Julia slowly brought it to her mouth. The smooth chocolate slid down her throat and soothed the hoarseness that had come from harsh words and tears. She looked at her mother over the top of her mug, trying her best to say *I'm sorry* with her eyes. Her mother gave a slight nod of her head and smiled at her daughter. Julia lowered her cup, and her mother and father began laughing.

"What's so funny?" Julia asked, careful not to use a defensive tone, just in case they really were her parents and not pod-people.

"Schnookums, you have a marshmallow mustache." Her dad laughed while reaching over and wiping her upper lip with his index finger. "See," he held the marshmallow covered finger up then quickly popped it in his mouth.

"Oh Dad, you are sooooo gross!" Julia giggled. *Nope, not pod-people. Only my dad would do something that disgusting,* Julia thought, taking another swig of cocoa.

Yeah! RB flapped her straps up and down. *My little buds get to be together and hopefully figure out how to give support to each other as they begin to emerge into blossoms!*

***

"Well," Annabelle said with a sigh after Julia closed the car door and ran up the walk to Sydney's, "I hope we handled that right. I don't want Julia to think she can get away with yelling at me, but I'm not so old that I don't remember the turmoil I felt as a tween."

Jon took his hand off the steering wheel and reached over and gave Annabelle a gentle squeeze on her thigh. "She'll be fine dear, just watch. She'll come home tomorrow all full of smiles. We still have our little girl."

Julia ran up the walk and rang the doorbell. Sydney and Riley raced to the door, sliding the last few feet in their stocking feet and crashing into the door. Sydney opened the door, her cheeks flush from the mad dash and the ensuing collision.

"Yeah!" Sydney cried, "You made it!" The girls began jumping up and down, excited to be spending the night together.

Julia took off her Nikes and put them by the front door with the other shoes.

"Here, give me your stuff," Sydney said, grabbing Julia's duffle bag and pillow.

"I see you brought Frita," Riley said with a grin.

"Yeah, well it's Dorita tonight," Julia said, reaching over and patting her pillow. "Frita's twin sister."

The girls giggled uncontrollably each with their memories of Julia and her pillow.

Julia always brought her pillow to every sleepover. When they were in third grade, they decided to name her pillow. They chose Frita because someone had spilled a bag of Fritos, covering the pillow with flecks of crispy corn snacks and salt.

"Come on," Sydney said, I've got the Wii set up in the basement. Let's go do some bowling."

Sydney opened the door to her room on the way to the basement and tossed Julia's things on her bed. Sarah, hearing the girls, stepped out of the kitchen and met the girls as they reached the top of the basement stairs.

"Hi Julia, glad you could make it! One burger or two?"

"Hi, one is fine, thank you."

"Cheese or no cheese?"

"Cheese is good," Julia said giggling as Sydney grabbed her arm and drug her down the steps.

"Uh, bye," Julia said, struggling to maintain her balance.

Oh, to be young again, Sara thought as she headed outside to the deck to let Kyle know the final burger count.

The girls laughed their way through bowling, all three frequently talking at once.

Sarah hollered down from the top of the stairs, "Supper's almost ready!"

"K, Mom," Sydney shouted back. "We're in the eighth frame. Be up as soon as I make a turkey!"

"You're the turkey," Julia said, giving Sydney a gentle push as she was getting ready to throw her ball.

"Hey, no fair!" Sydney said, watching her ball on the screen slide into the gutter.

"Gobble, gobble," Riley said, putting her hands under her arms, squatting down, and waddling around the room.

Sydney, giggling and distracted by the turkey in the room, tossed her second ball into the gutter.

As Julia stood in front of the screen and began to take her turn, Sydney jumped in front of her, causing her ball to also land in the gutter.

"Supper's ready!" they heard Sara shout. "Come on girls, let's get 'em while they're hot!"

"I don't know about you, but I'm starving," Riley said.

"Yeah, me too," chimed in Julia as she laid her controller on the TV stand. "Bowling's hard work."

The girls raced up the steps to join Sydney's family for dinner.

THE RED BRA

I had no idea being young was so carefree, RB thought while slowly raising and lowering her straps. *But oh, these buds do make me smile.*

With dinner over the girls went to Sydney's room. Riley flopped on the bed while Julia landed in the pink beanbag chair, and Sydney sat on the chair by her desk.

"What do you wanna do?" Riley asked, punctuating the 'do' with a loud belch.

"Ewww," Julia moaned, "why did you let the moose out of the lodge?"

"Better than letting a skunk out of the barn," Riley said, rolling over on her stomach and attempting to blow onion breath towards Julia.

"Phew," Julia said, waving her hands in the air, "whatcha put so many onions on your burger for? I'm not sleeping next to you!"

"That was the plan," Riley said grinning.

"Hey, you wanna make some bracelets?" Sydney asked while picking up her rubber band bracelet kit that was lying on her desk.

"Sure," Julia said, getting up from the beanbag chair and walking over to the desk.

"Oh, cool, when did you get this?" Julia said, picking up one of the rubber bands from the "Shimmer and Sparkle" kit.

"My grandma got it for me. Look, you can add beads."

Riley got up from the bed and walked over to her friends. "Oh, snap! I bet Sophia doesn't have any of these bracelets with beads."

"Well," Julia said, "I guarantee you if we go to school wearing these with beads in them, Sophia will come to school the next day wearing twenty of 'em all full of beads!"

Sydney rolled her eyes. "What's with her anyway? Trying to get me to invite her. *I can bring my Ouija board, I have Despicable Me, I have a blue ray, I can bring a thousand outfits,*" Sydney said, mimicking Sophia's voice.

"And don't forget the scarlet bra," Riley said dryly.

"What the heck color is scarlet anyway?" Sydney asked.

Julia, busy picking through the rubber bands held up a bright red band and flung it at Sydney.

"That, my dear," she said using the best hoity-toity voice she could manage, "is scarlet."

Riley began laughing as Sydney said, "Speaking of bras..."

"Ooh, ooh," Riley said, her laughter now turned to excitement, "let me see your bras! Oh, Julia, I don't think I told you, Mom said I could get one!"

"Uh, really, you gonna get a scarlet one?" she said, flinging another red rubber band, this time in Riley's direction. "Or are you gonna get a blue one?" she said, flinging a blue rubber band. "Or maybe a green one," she began as she flung a green rubber band.

"Cut it out, Julia," Sydney said, bending down and picking up the rubber bands.

"What!" Julia said, turning to face Sydney. "What colors do you have?" she said, starting to admit to herself that she was just a little curious about them.

Sydney walked over to her drawer and pulled out her pink and gray sport bras.

"These are called sport bras. They come in all sizes. High school and college girls even wear them. My sister has some. She says they are good for when you're playing basketball and stuff. Mom said they would be good beginner bras for me." She held up the pink bra with the blue trim.

"Kinda cute," Riley said.

"Just looks like a chopped off tank top to me," Julia said.

"Yeah," Sydney said, "I guess it sort of does." She tossed it to Julia.

"Eww," Julia said, dodging the bra heading her way. "I don't want to touch that – it's been on your boobies."

"Good grief, Julia," Riley said, bending over and picking up the bra. "I think it's been washed, and even if it wasn't, haven't you worn Sydney's shirts before? What's the big deal!"

"Yeah," Sydney said, opening her closet door and grabbing the bra she had earlier wrangled from the bottom of the laundry basket. She threw it at Julia while laughing, "now *this* one… not so clean."

Julia dodged the bra as Riley reached her hand out and intercepted it.

"Well, la-de-da, what's this?" she said, scooping her finger under the bra strap and twirling it around.

"Stop it, give it here," Sydney said, trying to grab the bra from Riley.

"Nope, mine now," she said grinning. She quit spinning the bra and held it in front of her chest and began to strut around the room like a runway model.

"And this, ladies and gentlemen, is the brassiere all the ladies are dyyying to have," Riley chortled as she pranced around the room.

Sydney began laughing, and Julia couldn't help but grin also.

RB rapidly flapped her straps up and down in delight. *What fun! Oh, I love, love, love these girls!*

Riley sat down on the bed and looked closely at the bra. It was white with small lightly padded cups surrounded by lace. A tiny pink heart was sewn in the middle of the cups. Unable to squelch her curiosity, Julia moved over to the bed and sat by Riley.

"What's this one for? Your wedding?" Julia said with a smirk.

"Oh my god, Julia, haven't you ever even looked at bras?"

Julia thought for a second, "Uh, no, can't say I have."

"Not even your mom's?"

"No, ewww."

"Well, don't you help with the laundry?" Riley asked. "I always have to fold the laundry. I hate touching my mom's panties," she shuddered when she said the word panties. "I touch them as little as possible."

The girls giggled, imagining Riley picking up her mother's panties with her pinky and tossing them in her dresser drawer.

"Mom just thought I would like to have, you know, a pretty bra, for wearing to church and stuff."

"What's with the padding?" Riley asked, feeling the fabric in the cup.

"It just gives a smoother look to my dresses. I don't know, makes me feel grown up when I wear it."

"You mean it makes you look like you have hooters," Julia said snickering.

"No," Sydney said, starting to get irritated at Julia. "Feel it." She grabbed the bra from Riley and tossed it to Julia.

Julia knew she was starting to tick off Sydney and figured she had better cool it. She caught the bra and felt the fabric in the cup. "Yeah, it's nice," she said, tossing it back to Sydney. *Hmm,* Julia thought to herself. *I bet my lopsided titties wouldn't show with a bra like that.*

"You got any more?" Riley asked.

"Just the one I'm wearing. It's just a regular training bra. It's the one you saw in PE." She lifted her blouse to show the girls. "See," she said, turning around and trying to bunch her T-shirt up in the back so they could see the back of the bra. "No hooks. It just slips over your head like the sports bras, but it has cups and adjustable straps."

"You call those cups?" Julia snorted, regretting the words as soon as they were out of her mouth.

"What is your problem?" Sydney angrily said turning to face Julia. "Your mom told me she said you could get a bra so get over it already and just get one!"

Julia glared at Sydney, fighting back the tears that were starting to form.

Sydney put her hand over her mouth, "Oh my god, Julia, I'm sorry. Your mom didn't mean to tell me. It's just, she was at my house when I got home, and I was telling my mom that Riley's mom said she could get a bra, and your mom said you could get one and...."

Riley interrupted, "You told your mom *and* Julia's mom I was going to get a bra?"

"I'm sorry," Sydney said, the tears now starting to pool in her eyes. "I was just excited. Sydney wiped her eyes with the heel of her hand. Come on, let's not fight. I thought it would be fun for us all to try on my bras, and I figured maybe we could all go bra shopping together."

Oh no! RB thought, her straps dropping below her cups. *Maybe they aren't emotionally ready for bud holders.*

The girls, sitting silently, glared at Sydney. Then as quickly as the fuss began, it ended when Riley jumped up and whipped off her T-shirt, exposing her bare chest and emerging buds.

RB's straps shot straight up, she pushed out her cups and laughed joyously. You go, Riley! Yes, my young ladies are ready to begin their journey into bra-dom and womanhood!

Julia stood, her mouth gaped open.
"What? Give me that bra, Sydney."
Sydney handed her the bra and Julia backed up and fell into the bean bag chair, not taking her eyes off Riley's chest.
Riley slipped the straps over her shoulders, the cups hanging loosely over her buds.
"Uh," Julia said, still staring at Riley's chest. "What's that brown thing below your boob?"
"Oh, that. It's my third nipple," Riley said matter of factly as she held the bra over her breasts.
"You're what?" Sydney asked bending down eye level with Riley's chest to get a better look.
Julia sat still, too flabbergasted to say anything.
"You've seen it before, Sydney."
"I thought it was a mole or something."
"My Grandma has one too. She said one in fifty women have them. She said it makes me special. I think they're called supernummy or something like that. Hey, did you know Harry has four nipples?"

"No way!" Sydney said, backing up and sitting down on the edge of the bed.

"Yeah, google it, you can even see pictures," Riley said as she struggled with trying to clasp the bra behind her back. "How do you get this darn thing on anyway?"

"Oh geez," Sydney said. "You hook it in front, then you twist it to the back and put your arms in the straps."

Riley gave her a quizzical look. "Huh?"

"Take it off, and wrap it around your chest under your uh,"

"Boobs," Julia interjected.

"Your breasts," Sydney said, casting a sour glance at Julia.

Riley did as she was told.

"No, wrap it with the clasp in front so you can see it to hook it."

"Oh, duh," Riley turned the bra around and began fiddling with the hooks. "How come there are so many hooks? Which ones do I use?"

"Whichever one makes it feel, I don't know, the right tightness. Not too tight, not too loose." Riley chose the middle hooks. After hooking the bra together, she turned it around and slipped the straps over her arms. The cups gaped, and Julia began laughing.

"What are you laughing at?" Riley asked, "I don't see you trying one on."

"Here," Sydney said, grabbing a handful of tissues from the bedside table. "Shove these in there."

Riley laughed raucously as she stuffed her bra full of tissues. Once again, she began her model routine, prancing around the room while saying, "Now, ladies and gentlemen, for only one dollar more, you can have a box of tissues to round out your bra."

Sydney laughed as Julia, still lounging in the bean bag chair, began thinking about her lopsided problem. *I can't believe it doesn't bother Riley that she has three nipples,* she thought. *That's worse than having two different sized boobs.* Julia continued to mull it over in her mind. *Oh, what the heck.*

"Sydney, can I try on the gray sport bra?"

"Sure, if you aren't afraid you'll get cooties," she laughed before tossing the bra to Julia.

Julia looked at the bra then looked at her besties. They were busy stuffing more tissues in Riley's bra. Julia stood up and turned with her back to the girls. Quickly, she pulled off her T-shirt. Glancing behind her she saw Riley shoving one of the tissues up her nose as Sydney fell to the floor laughing. Julia quickly pulled off the tank top she was wearing beneath her T-shirt and slid the sport's bra over her head.

Sydney looked up from the floor at Julia. "Awesome! It fits you perfectly! You should get some of these."

Riley picked the tissue from her nose and faced Julia. Julia noted that now Riley's boobs were really lopsided and lumpy too. She giggled and pointed at Riley's overflowing bra.

"Ta-da!" Riley said, jumping in the air and landing with her feet spread and her hands forming a V above her head.

"You're crazy," Julia said.

"You got that right," Riley said, lolling her tongue out of the corner of her mouth and crossing her eyes. She straightened up and said, "Cool bra, Julia, you should get some like that."

Julia looked down at her chest, surprised the girls hadn't commented on the size difference. *Maybe it's not so bad,* she thought as she caught a glimpse of herself in the mirror and saw her image smiling back. *Not so bad at all.*

Well, I'll be, RB lifted herself high and straightened her straps and cups. *It looks like my little buds got it all figured out on their own. They are going to be such beautiful flowers one day! I think it's time for me to move on.*

Chapter 6
High School

RB lifted herself and sailed towards the setting sun, twisting and turning with the subtle breezes that wafted through the evening sky. She floated throughout the night, relishing the crisp, dry air, and thrilled that for once she bore no sweat stains. When the sun began its ascent from beneath the horizon, she started paying more attention to the world below her. Hearing the shrill sound of whistles and boys grunting and panting, she paused. *This may be interesting*, she thought while venturing closer to land. *Oh, my, football practice! I do like to admire strong, young virile bodies,* she mused, closing in on the view below.

"Tweet!" the coach's whistle screeched through the morning air. "You pussies! Is that all you can do? Come on! Let's try it again, and this time hit somebody!" Coach spat on the ground and scribbled furiously in his notepad before raising his head to continue his tirade. "Derrick, get your head down! Come on, show me what ya got!"

"Geez," Derrick said to Collin as they were walking up to the line of scrimmage, "what's his problem?"

"Probably didn't get any this morning," Collin responded. Carrying the ball to the line and getting in position. "Hut, hut," he shouted as the ball flew out of his hand towards Derrick. Still processing his remark, Derrick barely grasped the ball. He stepped back, faked a pass to the right, held his head down, and barreled straight through the defensive line. His broad shoulders and six-foot-one frame made it easy for him to push through the line. He was second string lineman for varsity his freshman year and first string his sophomore year while also starting every game on the junior varsity team. Now, a two hundred and five-pound junior with the strength, speed, and agility of a gazelle, Coach was testing his skills as a quarterback. Derrick took it all in stride. He loved the game, and as long as he could play, the position was not an issue to him.

"Tweet!" Once again, the coaches shrill whistle blasted through the crisp fall air. "Showers!" coaches booming voice yelled.

Derrick and Collin pulled off their helmets and trotted to the locker room.

"Good play, pussy," Collin jokingly laughed at Derrick when they entered the locker room.

"Yeah, whatever," Derrick said pulling off his practice jersey and pads before heading for the showers. Standing still with his face raised upward, he felt the cool water wash over his body while his mind wandered to first hour and Jessica. Jessica. *She sure is beautiful*, he thought, envisioning her sitting across from her in world history class. He turned the cold water on full blast and let it run over his curly blond hair. *Geez,* he thought to himself, *get a grip. You've known her since kindergarten. Why this sudden obsession?* Stepping out of the shower, he grabbed a towel walked to the locker area. The room was engulfed with the smell of sweat and the sounds of towels snapping and boys jeering at one another.

"Hey, Joe," Michael yelled across the room. "Get any of that sweet meat from Kim lately?"

"Nah," Joe hollered back, "been too busy doin' your mom!"

"Ooooh – someone's gonna get their ass kicked," Brad snickered.

Michael puffed himself up and shook his fist at Joe. "One of these days, boy, one of these days!"

"Come on guys," Derrick said, "we got to get to class. You know how pissed coach gets when we get tardy slips."

"Aww, is Derrick scared of da coach?" Michael shot back.

Derrick finished tying his shoes and threw his backpack over his shoulder. "I'm outta here. Grow up, would ya."

Michael turned towards Brad, "What's up his ass?"

"Aww, he just wants to get to class early to see Jessica."

"Oh, snap! Since when did he get interested in anything besides football?"

"Since Jessica started growing tits!"

Brad took his hands and shoved his breasts together and began prancing around the locker room. "Oh, boys, look at me – look at me – I have titties now – look at meeeeee!" He chortled in a high-pitched voice.

Michael burst out laughing, spit and snot flying across the room.

"Oh, yeah, you're the man," said Brad. "Every girl wants a guy that can blow snot five feet from his nose."

Ew, I'm so glad I never had to go into a locker room! RB thought as she watched the boys continue to throw barbs back and forth. *Shame on them for making fun of that young woman and her blossoming breasts! All except Derrick. Hmm, he just might be one of the good ones. I think I'll follow him for a bit. Besides, I'm kind of curious about this Jessica.*

Chapter 7
Derrick

Derrick strolled down the halls of Lincoln High School, glad to be back in school after a long summer of working on his family's farm. He liked the solitude of running the combine and the labor of baling hay, but he didn't like the long hours. Walking down the hall, he reminisced about his heritage and the stories his grandpa told him about how the Murphy family had worked the Iowa ground for as long back as there were records. They began with five hundred acres and now had close to three thousand. They grew wheat, corn, and soybeans. Black gold, his grandpa called the land they owned. Derrick loved the smell of the rich, fertile soil. He enjoyed listening to his grandpa's stories; the drought during the fifties, combines with no air conditioning or radios, and shooting coons and groundhogs that feasted on his crops. He stopped to get a drink from the water fountain and thought about how much he missed his grandpa. He passed on when Derrick was twelve. He was still young enough to enjoy sitting on the front porch and listen to his grandpa's yammering. Derrick had two older brothers and an older sister. He knew he was lucky to be allowed to play football. His older brothers didn't get the privilege since they needed to be available to work on the farm during practice hours and game times. His mother was approaching her fiftieth birthday when he was born, and by the time he was old enough to help with the farming they had hired hands and his help wasn't as critical as it was when his brothers were his age. His dad was now seventy-two, and his mom was sixty-six. They had slowed down and mellowed a bit in their age, but his dad still drove the tractor, and his mom still put in a big garden and canned green beans and tomatoes every summer. It was his oldest brother, Darnell, who convinced their dad to let him play. Darnell was much older than Derrick that at times it was more like having another father than having an older brother. Darnell had a son and another one on the way when Derrick was born. He wasn't old school like their dad, and sometimes Derrick wondered if he resented that his youth was spent baling hay and driving tractors and combines instead of playing football and hanging out with friends like he did. *Not that I hang out much with friends,* Derrick thought, nearing his locker. *Or know what they're talking about half the time,* he thought while watching kids leaning against their lockers with their heads bent over the screens of their phones, their fingers dancing across the tiny keyboard that he couldn't imagine doing. He knew his parents were of a different era, and he respected that. He didn't bother them about getting a computer. The only reason he had a cell phone was because Darnell put him on their family plan, but he didn't text much. Shaking his head, he stood and backed away from the water fountain. Quickening his pace, he recalled how Jessica had pretty much been his only friend growing up. He knew her because her family farmed the ground down the road from them. They were in 4-H together, showing off their lop-eared rabbits and the occasional goat or sheep they raised. They also both attended St. Mary's Catholic School through junior high, but being farm kids, they were frequently taunted by the other children. Kids would hold their noses when they walked by and make pig noises. Neither of them ever raised pigs, so they would laugh and keep on walking. They rode the same bus to school for the first nine years of their education. They were the first ones on the bus and the last ones off. Since Derrick's siblings were out on their own, Jessica became more like a surrogate sister than anything. He would pull on her pigtails, and she would punch him in the arm.

Things changed when high school began, and they were thrown into the chaos of public education along with every race, creed, and economic status. Jessica had attended tumbling classes in grade school and dance classes in junior high. She had made friends who weren't of the Catholic faith before attending public school which meant she had friends from the get-go. They picked her up for school before she got her license while Derrick continued to ride the bus until he could legally drive. Being raised on a farm, he had begun driving when he was old enough for his feet to touch the pedals and his head to see through the windshield. Once he turned sixteen, his dad let him drive the old Ford pickup truck to school. Derrick wasn't a proud sort of guy, but he did feel embarrassed when he would pull up next to the Camaros and Mustangs complete with spoilers and sound systems that would cause a suckling ewe to pull away from his mama.

Derrick arrived at his locker as the warning bell rang. He grabbed his world history book, notebook, and pens and headed to class. It was the second week of school, and he was anxious to get to class and see Jessica. He walked into class and flopped down in his seat, stretching his long legs out as far as he could without bumping the seat in front of him. He didn't get why Mr. Johnson insisted on assigned seats even though the majority of the class were juniors and seniors, but he was glad because he knew at least one period of the day he was guaranteed that he could look out the corner of his eye and see her. She was also in his Spanish II class, but Senorita Gonzales never paid any attention to where anyone sat which meant some days they sat close enough to talk, and other days she was across the room from him.

Derrick looked over at Jessica. "Hey."

"Hay is for horses, grass is cheaper," Jessica replied referring to the dialogue of their younger days.

"Got me there."

Jessica, wearing a scooped neck red blouse with a white tank underneath threw a big smile towards him. Seeing her cleavage peeking out from the top of her tank top, his cheeks turned crimson red. *God, when did she turn in to a Hustler centerfold,* he thought while feeling the flush warming his face. He turned his head and opened his notebook, furiously trying not to picture her naked.

Oh, boy! RB exclaimed throwing back her straps and inwardly laughing. *Gotta love that red blouse, but mercy me, her girls are trying to escape! Poor Derrick!*

"So," began Jessica, oblivious to his flushed state, "I hear you're trying out for quarterback this year."

Lordy, Derrick thought to himself, *word sure does travel quickly around here.*

"Umm, maybe," he said, keeping his eyes focused on his notes.

Jessica turned in her seat to face him, resting her elbows on her legs, her hands cupping her chin and causing the plump curves of her breasts to push the limits of her blouse.

"That's great. Bet Darnell is proud of you."

"Uh, I haven't told him yet."

"What? Come on Derr, you know he would be like, oh yeah, that's my bro, NFL next stop!" Jessica sat up and brushed her long dark hair behind her head.

Her infectious laugh bubbled forth from her slender lips, and his head began to swim. He had no idea why, but her laugh had been making things in his body twinge before he knew what twinges were all about. All he knew for sure was from the first time in seventh grade when they were partnered up for a science experiment that involved – what was it? He tried to remember as he concentrated on keeping his eyes averted from her chest. Watching food coloring swirl around a bowl of warm milk and soap? Yeah, that was it. Something or another about how matter always moved. Mrs. Claybourne, their science teacher, was walking around the room reminding everyone not to touch the table. He recalled her telling everyone to control their variables, and he remembered Joe getting chastised for blowing on the experiment. Derrick grinned when he recalled Jessica pretending to blow once Mrs. Claybourne passed their desk. They were stifling their giggles when Jessica's pencil slipped through her fingers and landed on the floor by his feet. He quickly bent down to pick it up before Mrs. Claybourne noticed anything affecting their variables. Jessica bent at the same time. Their heads knocked, and with their heads bent over so close together – he first noticed not only the knocking of their heads – but her knockers...

"Earth to Derrick," whispered Jessica.

Derrick shook himself out of his reverie, and Jessica nodded towards the front of the room. Mr. Johnson was standing at his podium in the front of the class. "Everyone, and I mean EVERYONE, can I please have your attention," he stated in his booming voice.

Jessica, turning to face the teacher, opened her history book to the page dictated by the numbers written on the board. She tried to concentrate on the state of the world in 1942, but frankly, how did the Japanese taking Guadalcanal have anything to do with her? she wondered. Sneaking a glance at Derrick studiously taking notes, a wave of admiration came over her. She knew he gave his due diligence to every task at hand and aspired to be successful in every aspect of his life. He was her best friend, but she didn't think he knew. Who else in this world would wipe cow crap off her when she slipped and fell at the county fair and not tell anyone? That was a turning point for her. They were in the fifth grade. They had been in 4-H together since kindergarten. That year she had a goat named Charley that she entered in the fair, and Derrick entered his rabbit, Fester. They both earned blue ribbons, and boy were they proud. After the ribbons were presented, Derrick was carrying his rabbit cage back to his brother's pickup truck while she led Charley on his leash. They were walking between the stalls that housed the heifers when she hit a slick spot and went flailing. All she remembered was losing the leash and yelling out for Derrick to get Charley while she did a backslide through a humongous pile of cow dung.

He could have laughed, he could have made all kinds of 'crappy' jokes, but he didn't. He scooped up Charley's leash as it landed in the dung while balancing Fester's cage with his free arm. He set Fester and his cage down, tied up Charley to a nearby post, and with the most concern she had ever seen in anyone's eyes, he lifted her from the muck, impervious to the smell, and no concern for the soiled mess that was now also covering his body. She tried not to cry, she really did, but tears of embarrassment and pain were too strong to stop the river of tears from flowing down her face. He put her arm over his shoulder and limped her over to the watering spigot at the end of the cattle pen. He tore off his t-shirt, pumped water on it, and used it to wipe the stench of what seemed like a hundred cow patties off her face, her arms, and her legs.

They never spoke a word. He cleaned her up, threw his soiled t-shirt over his shoulder, gathered Charley and Festus, and they slowly walked to his brother's truck. That day was never mentioned, but it was cataloged forever in Jessica's brain as one of the nicest things anyone had ever done for her.

"Jessica, what do you think?" Mr. Johnson's droll voice interrupted her thoughts.

"Um, sure, I agree with what you said," she meekly replied.

Laughter erupted in sporadic speckles around the classroom, and her cheeks turned bright red.

"Are you back with us, Miss Lewis?"

"Um, yes, could you please repeat the question?"

"What contributed to the Japanese defeat?"

Derrick coughed loudly while quickly scribbling FOOD in large words on his notebook and slanting it towards Jessica.

Looking at Derrick, Jessica blurted out, "Food!"

"And," he briefly paused, "what about food, Miss Lewis?"

"Well, they needed food, and…" she hung her head, embarrassed because she had no idea when Derrick spoke out.

"What I think she is trying to say is that the Japanese did not adequately supply their troops with sustenance, and this contributed to their defeat."

"Why, yes, Derrick, you are correct. Perhaps you could plan some study time with Jessica, so you don't have to waste an entire sheet of paper with one word. You know, our trees are a valuable resource."

Turning to the board, Mr. Johnson began writing a timeline of the events at Guadalcanal. Jessica mouthed *sorry* to Derrick. Shrugging his shoulders, he grinned before turning his attention to the board. *As always,* she thought, *Derrick to the rescue.*

Grabbing Derrick's arm as they were leaving class, Jessica said, "Hey, thanks for trying to help me out."

"No problem. That class can get pretty boring. I don't blame you for zoning out."

"Yeah, but Derrick, trees are such a valuable resource. You wasted a twig on me!"

"Funny girl, try to save your butt, and you're more concerned about saving trees."

Jessica punched him gently on the arm and flung her head to the side, her long dark hair gently falling in cascades around her face.

"Uh," Derrick began, looking towards his Converses, "you want to study together for the history test?" Wiping a bead of sweat off his upper lip, he raised his head and darted his eyes sideways glancing at her. *Dang,* he thought, *why is she having this effect on me?*

"Sure, wanna come to my house this weekend?"

"Yeah, sure, Derrick said, standing tall and looking intently at the top of her head. How about Sunday after church?"

"That should work. I'll let you know. See you soon."

Derrick tried to conceal the grin that was spreading over his face as Jessica walked away. Approaching his locker, he grabbed his books for lit class. Walking into class, he felt like he was floating on a cloud. Sliding into his desk and stretching his long legs forward he accidentally bumped the seat of Missy Greer. Quickly turning her head towards Derrick, her blond hair bounced off her shoulders. She flipped her hair back from her face and coyly looked Derrick in the eye.

"Hey, Derrick," she said in the sultriest voice she could manage. "If you wanted my attention all you had to do was say hey, not kick me," she giggled in a sophomoric tone.

Geez, not this again, Derrick thought. *Why does she think being a cheerleader makes her irresistible to all the football players? From what I heard in the locker room, she doesn't resist much.*

"Uh, sorry, just stretching," Derrick mumbled.

"So," Missy cooed, turning completely around in her desk. "You goin' to Collin's party this weekend?"

"Yeah, maybe, probably."

"Well," Missy said, flashing a seductive smile, "I'll see you there."

Ooh, I'll have to keep an eye on this girl, RB said, perusing the scene below her. *Maybe I'll finally get to see some action!*

94

Missy gave him a sly grin and turned back around in her seat. *Oh, how I would like to pluck that cherry she thought to herself* as she flipped her hair back causing the papers on Derrick's desk to flutter.

Derrick looked up from his papers as Missy's blonde hair floated over the top of them.

Staring at the back of her head, he watched it bob up and down. Derrick smirked, wondering if it were a silent tune causing her head to bob or all the air in it. He didn't see the appeal the other guys saw in the blue-eyed blondes that flirted shamelessly with most of the football team. He recalled when Mason, the lumbering three-hundred and twenty-pound linebacker, was shamelessly flirted with by several cheerleaders after a winning game. Mason came swaggering into the locker room the next morning for practice whistling a tune and trying to two-step his way around the benches. The guys whistled with him, and at him while giving him high five's. For a hulk of a guy, he sure was light on his toes that day.

Derrick catcalled and cajoled with the rest of the guys that day in the locker room, but inside he felt shame for Mason and shame for the girls who thought sex was some sort of game. He was a virgin in all ways. It wasn't a fact he admitted to the guys, but still, it was a fact. He knew there were girls who would be with him, but he had always been more reserved than most of the guys his age. He spent so much time working on the farm that he never developed the comfort level most kids had when interacting with others. He also took his Catholic upbringing seriously and wanted to wait for the girl he would marry.

"Ahem, Mr. Murphy, are you with us?" Derrick snapped out of his reverie and turned his attention to Mr. Jacobs.

Geez, Derrick thought, *how do these teachers always know when you're not paying attention?*

Derrick quickly opened *Of Mice and Men* to the chapter they had completed the day before. He was glad it was Friday and was looking forward to the scrimmage after school. Coach was putting him in as quarterback. He hoped Darnell would be able to come. He also hoped Jessica would be there.

After a quick review, Mr. Jacobs assigned pages to read silently, as he did every Friday. Missy once more flipped her long blond hair back in an effort to make Derrick notice her before she opened her book and stared blankly at the pages. *What do I have to do to get him to notice me?* She bleakly thought. She wondered if he remembered second grade when she attended the Catholic school and was in his class. *That was the year of, what was his name?* She tried to remember. *Oh, yeah, Tim. Or was it Tony?* Her mother had many different live-in boyfriends through the years it was hard for her to keep track of them all. She never knew her father, and when she questioned her mother, she always said all that mattered was that she was her mother. When Missy grew older, she realized her mother probably had no clue who her father was. Tim/Tony attended Catholic school when he was in grade school, and he felt Missy should also attend. Missy smiled at the vague memory. He was one of the nice ones. But, like all the nice ones, he didn't last long, so neither did her education in a private school. Rifling the corner of her book, she remembered the time Derrick shared one of his home-made chocolate chip cookies with her during lunch. She still remembered how good it tasted. Her mother never baked anything homemade.

Missy sighed before turning and sneaking a glance at Derrick. He was engrossed in the story in front of him. He was nice to her when they were little. He even shared his crayons when she couldn't find hers. She glanced at the clock, then back down at her book. *Thirty minutes left in the period. Guess I better start reading,* she thought, *cuz I really don't want to read this crap over the weekend.*

I wish she would leave me alone, Derrick thought, blowing on one of her hairs that had left her head and landed on his book with her last hair whooshing. He watched the hair float silently off his book and land on his desk beside his hand. *I wonder what happened to that shy little girl I knew in second grade,* he mused before turning a page. *I don't understand girls who throw themselves at guys. Now, Jessica,* he grinned as he thought her name. *I wish I could figure out if she would be interested in being more than a friend. She definitely doesn't throw herself at me, but then again, she isn't the same type of girl as Missy.*

Chapter 8
Missy

Missy was excited about the scrimmage which would be taking place that evening. She had made the cheer-leading squad and had spent endless hours in her room practicing their routines. She was glad her next-door neighbor and friend, Carolyn, had talked her into trying out. They were as different in personality as they were in looks, but their friendship remained strong throughout the years. Carolyn, with her short black hair and deep brown eyes, had a quiet, gentle demeanor. She knew Missy's mother had a carousel of men drifting in and out of Missy's life, but they never talked about it. Her own mother worried about Missy and frequently encouraged her to have her over for meals or to hang out. Carolyn's older sister, Rebecca, had been a cheerleader in high school, and a cheerleader at the University of California. Carolyn had been extremely proud of her and wanted to excel at cheer-leading just like her sister. While still in grade school she would spend hours watching her sister's routines and learning the cheers. It was a given that she would follow in her footsteps and make the squad herself once she entered high school. As predicted, Carolyn made the squad her freshman year, and Rebecca came home from college to watch her cheer her first game. Missy, too, had looked up to Rebecca through the years of being neighbors and friends, and she had learned many of the cheers before she entered high school. It was Carolyn's mother, Joan, who ultimately convinced Missy to try out. It saddened Missy to think Rebecca would never get to see her cheer.

Missy stood in front of the full-length mirror attached to her bedroom closet door and pulled her hair back in a ponytail. As she was tying blue and white ribbons around her hair, her mother poked her head in the door.

"How's my little cheer-leader doing?" her mother, Christy, asked with what Missy thought was a too cheerful voice.

"I'm a little nervous."

"Well," Christy said walking over and adjusting the bow on Missy's pony-tail, "no need to be. I've seen you practice; you'll be the shining star!"

Missy rolled her eyes, wondering when her mother ever watched her practice her cheers. She was either busy working at the beauty shop or busy working on her own personal beauty, so she could go man-hunting.

"Game starts at seven, Ma. It costs a bar of soap to get in."

"A bar of soap? What are you talkin' about?"

"It's a soap scrimmage. You know, a chance for the guys to have a practice game with an audience before the season starts. You pay with a bar of soap so, I don't know, so they have something to wash with after the games."

Christy laughed the deep throaty laugh she mainly used when she was man hunting.

What is her problem? Missy wondered.

"Ok. If I can scrounge up a bar of soap, I'll be there. Does it have to be a new bar?"

Missy glared at her mother.

"Just kidding, just kidding," she said, turning and walking out of the room.

Missy turned back to face the mirror and applied an extra layer of mascara to her already heavily made-up face. *She won't be there,* Missy thought. *Good, I don't want her there. Since she is currently between men, she would probably hit on the principal or something.* "Gross," she said out loud, a visual of her mother flirting flashing before her eyes. Picking up her bright red lipstick she carefully applied a fresh coat. She stood back and looked at herself. *Not bad,* she thought, reaching her hands into her bra and adjusted the girls for maximum cleavage.

Ewww-E! Check out the cleavage on Missy! I must say, she does know how to show off her assets! RB commented while observing Missy.

Walking out of her room, Missy entered the living room where her mother was lying on the couch flipping through an old issue of *People* magazine she had absconded from the beauty shop.

"Carolyn's giving me a ride to the game."

"K, hon," Christy said without looking up.

"Kick-off at seven."

"Uh, huh," Christy replied, flipping a page. "Have fun."

Missy walked out the door and slammed it hard.

Why do I even bother? she thought. *Like it would kill her to come watch her only kid do something.*

Missy walked across the yard towards Carolyn's house. *I don't give a shit. I really don't,* she thought, knocking on Carolyn's door.

Carolyn's dad, Jeff, answered the door. He was a big man, with a big heart, and an even bigger smile erupted on his face when he saw Missy at the door.

"Well, looky here, we've got us another cheer-leader!" Jeff exclaimed opening the door wide.

"Joan!" He hollered to his wife with his booming voice. "Come look at little Missy!"

Joan walked towards the entryway carrying a dishtowel and wiping her hands.

"Well, just look at you!" she beamed. "Aren't you the most precious thing!"

Missy did a quick curtsy and with a big smile said, "Aww, thanks." Sometimes she didn't know how to respond to the praises the Browne family frequently lavished on her.

"Carolyn is in her room. You know where it is," Joan smiled while reaching out and brushing a stray hair from Missy's face.

Missy walked into Carolyn's room. She was standing with her back to the door. Her torso was naked except for her bra which was wrapped around her middle, the cups dangling loosely below her breasts, the straps brushing her sides. Missy could see Carolyn fiddling with something; her head bent towards her breasts.

"What the heck are you doing, girl?" Missy asked, walking over and standing in front of Carolyn.

Carolyn laughed and showed Missy a band-aid that was folded over and stuck to itself.

Missy looked at the band-aid wrappers scattered on the floor and gave her friend a puzzled look.

"I'm trying to cover my nipples, and I must be a moron because I can't even unwrap a band-aid!"

"Okayyyy," Missy said, still puzzled by the band-aids. "Did you cut yourself or something?"

"No, you goof. I need to cover my nipples, so they don't show through my top. It's probably gonna be chilly this evening, and I don't need my nipples sticking out for the world to see."

Laughing, Missy said, "You have got to be joking!"

Carolyn lifted her head and stared directly into Missy's eyes. "No, I'm not. Some people don't like the world to look at their ta-tas," she said lowering her eyes to Missy's cleavage and back up to Missy's eyes.

"Hey, you got it, you flaunt it," Missy replied placing her hands below her breasts and giving them a slight push causing them to bulge even further over the top of her V-neck cheer-leading top.

You go, girl! RB shimmied her cups while watching Missy. *That's one way to get attention. Assuming it's your boobs you want to give the attention.*

"Here," Missy said with an exasperated tone. Reaching towards the table, she picked up a fresh band-aid. Missy opened the band-aid and stripped off the tabs. She stuck one side to her finger, the band-aid dangling straight as she flashed it before Carolyn.

Carolyn grabbed the band-aid and stuck it over her nipple.

"Guess you need another one, huh," Missy said with a grin.

Carolyn stuck her tongue out at her while Missy expertly unwrapped another band-aid and handed it to her.

Missy sat down on the bed as Carolyn adjusted her bra and slipped on her cheer-leading top. "You know," she began with a sly grin. "There are exercises you can do to make your boobs bigger."

"And who says I want bigger boobs?" Carolyn drolly replied.

"Oh, *everyone* wants bigger boobs," Missy said. Jumping up from the bed, she put her hands on her hips and spread her legs in her best cheerleader's pose. "Ah-hmm," she said. "Time for me to teach *you* a cheer. Missy put her palms together in front of her breasts with her fingers lying over her wrists. She winked at Carolyn, a little something from Judy Blume and me to you. "One, two, three," Missy began, pushing her palms together to the beat of her count and causing her breasts to jiggle with every beat. She continued to press her palms together while belting out her cheer.

"The bust, the bust, we must increase the bust!
The bigger, the better, the tighter the sweater,
We must increase the bust!"

"Grow girls grow!" She finished her cheer with a jump and a fist pump to the air.

Carolyn giggled. "You are really insane; you know that?"

"Why thank you, but seriously, you need to do something about those little nubs of yours."

Carolyn ignored her comment with an eye roll. *I'm fine just the way I am,* she thought. *Besides, Becca was the one who got all the big boob genes.* Shaking her head, she put a smile on her face, remembering Becca reciting the same rhyme.

RB stirred, lifted her straps high and clapped her cups together in delight. *Oh, yes, you are just fine! But then again, that's what all the itty bitties say. But I guess you don't know what you're missing if you never had it to begin with!* RB shimmied her cups in rueful delight when suddenly, and without warning, her right strap fell, then the left strap fell, and her cups sagged. *The bigger, the better...* RB recited the words from the cheer, unsure of what she was feeling. Pausing for only a brief moment, she pushed her cups together, lifted them high, straightened her straps, and sighed before soaring off to the football field.

Chapter 9
Jessica

Jessica and her girlfriend, Treena, walked through the gate to the football field. Jessica handed off her bar of Coast deodorant soap to the attendant while Treena tossed her Zest over his head and into the bin.

"Think that'll keep 'em from stinkin'?" Treena asked, hooking her arm through Jessica's while surveying the crowd that was milling along the sidelines.

"We can only hope," Jessica said, smiling at her friend.

Jessica and Treena had been close friends during the elementary years when they both attended tumbling classes together. They didn't hang out much throughout the junior high years because they both quit tumbling by fifth grade. Since Treena attended public school, they didn't see much of each other after that. Now that they were both in high school, they were slowly rebuilding their friendship.

Jessica admired Treena's boldness, and at times wished she could be more like her. Although there were times she wished Treena would get a better filter for her mouth. Walking around the outskirts of the football field, Jessica reflected on some of the past embarrassing encounters that had occurred while around Treena and hoped this evening's events would not add to the list. Treena tended to say whatever she thought as soon as she thought it.

Loudly. Like the time she turned to her in the middle of algebra class and said her boobs were soooo sore she didn't think she could even touch them with a powder puff. And she didn't say it quietly. Their classmates turned to stare at both of them. Some chuckled, and some sneered and made snide comebacks. Treena just stared back at them and said, *What?? I'm on my period*, as Jessica slunk down in her seat and tried to become invisible. Mr. Wilson used his selective hearing to ignore them and continued to write equations on the board.

Jessica leaned her head back and took a deep breath of the fresh evening air, shoving the memories behind her. Arriving at the bleachers, they climbed to the top row where they joined a group of kids from school. Treena high-fived and fist-bumped her way through the rows of rowdy kids and Jessica meekly waved at a few. Treena never knew a stranger, and if someone she knew were talking to someone she didn't know, she would barge right up and introduce herself.

Jessica enjoyed watching the game and seeing Derrick tear through the line and make a first in ten. She jumped and cheered with the rest of the kids and liked feeling part of the in-crowd. She had many casual friends and felt like she fit in with most of the cliques, but she never felt like she belonged to any one group. Treena was part of the most popular clique, and that evening Jessica felt like she was starting to be accepted as one of them.

Hearing a loud laugh that was more of a snort, Jessica turned and glanced up at Treena, laughing wildly and standing with her back against the local hardware store ad which provided a backdrop for the top row of bleachers. Treena was bringing a flask to her mouth. She took a long drink. Chuck, who was standing beside her, reached for it as Treena was screwing the cap back on.

"Oh, no you don't," Treena giggled, pulling the flask close to her chest. The evening air was unseasonably warm, and Treena was wearing a light jacket over a V-neck sweater. Quickly, she slid the flask inside her opened jacket and tucked it into the V of her sweater, the silver cap protruding out between the curves of her breasts. Chuck reached his hand towards the now well-insulated flask as Treena twisted away preventing Chuck from removing it, but not before his hand grazed her breast. She stared at him with steely eyes, and his cheeks flushed. He quickly took a step back, tripping over some legs and barely keeping himself from tumbling down the bleachers. Treena's eyes took on a look of amusement, and she laughed. "I thought you wanted booze, not milk," she shouted at Chuck.

My, my Jessica is so right. That girl has no filter on her mouth! RB thought while watching the teens. *I wonder just what sort of game she's playing, shoving that flask up against her girls like that – taunting him. Hmpf. I think she wanted him to cop a feel.*

Treena, still laughing, hopped down a step and sat next to Jessica, pulling the flask out as she did. Handing it to

Jessica, she said, "Here, have a slug. You don't even have to touch my boob." A big grin erupted on her face as she offered the flask to Jessica.

"Uh, no thanks."

"Suit yourself," Treena said, slipping the flask in her jacket pocket. "So, Derrick's doing okay out there, huh?"

"What? Oh, I didn't notice."

Treena lightly elbowed her. "Yeah, right, when are you two gonna finally hook up? Chill already, you been hanging with him for what, your whole life?"

"Eww, it's not like that with us. He's more like a brother than anything."

"Yeah, a hot brother! Seriously, Jess, you should try to hook up with him before he gets Missy's germs all over him."

Jessica turned and looked at Treena, "What do you mean by that?"

"Well, after Lit class today I heard Missy say she was going to hook up with him at Collin's party. I did see her flirting with him in class. Maybe he's tired of waiting for your skinny ass to throw a bone his way, or should I say to let him throw his bone your way." Treena giggled. "Oh, I crack myself up!"

"He wouldn't do that. She's so full of BS." Jessica felt a knot in her stomach as she said the words. *Missy Greer, yuck. He wouldn't, would he? Why should I even care? It's not like I like him like **that**. Missy and her long blonde hair and big honkin' boobs. Gross.* She looked out towards the field where Missy and the other cheerleaders were jumping up and down and shouting first in ten, do it again. *She's just plain nasty.* Jessica thought to herself. *I remember when she was in our second-grade class. I thought she was an orphan. She was skinny as a rail, and her hair was always dirty and full of knots. Oh yeah, and she smelled like pee.* "Give me that bottle," Jessica said to Treena, reaching her hand towards Treena's jacket pocket.

"It's a flask, my dear, a flask," Treena said, taking it out of her pocket and handing it to Jessica.

"Whatever."

Jessica opened the lid and took a long swallow, the liquid burning its way down her throat.

"Hey, easy girl, save some for the second half," Treena said, grabbing the flask from Jessica's hand just as it was about to hit her lips for another swig. "Since when did you start drinking anyway? Think you can score any booze from your folk's stash for the party tomorrow night?"

"I don't drink, and no I can't swipe any booze."

"Uh, that was booze you just poured down your throat, so uh, yeah, maybe you didn't use to drink, but now you do. No do-overs in life – what's done is done, I say let's party on!" Treena did a double fist pump to the air while playfully bumping shoulders with Jessica.

Jessica felt the alcohol burning loose the knot in her stomach. *That wasn't too bad,* she thought, remembering the tiny glass of Mogen David her parents gave her last year during Easter dinner. Before then she had never drunk any alcohol, except communion wine. When her parents poured her the couple sips of wine she was surprised, and it made her feel grown up – until they prayed, and she realized it was just more communion wine. Still, she felt her parents were looking at her as more adult than a child.

"Oh, here," Treena said, handing the flask back to Jessica. "Have some more. Maybe it will put a smile on your face. By the way, it's Jack Daniels."

"You got it from Jack who?" Jessica asked, taking the bottle while staring at the sidelines and watching Missy jump up and down. *I hope her boobs are sore tomorrow,* she thought. *All that bouncing up and down. Geez, you'd think she'd get a better bra.*

Treena laughed. "What rock did you crawl out from under? Jack, Jack Daniels, it's the name of the whiskey you're drinking."

"Oh, yeah, right, I knew that,"

Treena followed Jessica's line of vision and saw she was staring at Missy.

Treena, too, stared at Missy flouncing up and down and rah-rah rahhing like she owned the place. *How the hell she made it on the squad I'll never know,* Treena thought. *Probably men judges, and she flashed them her tits.* Treena smirked at the thought.

"Bet she has ugly nipples," Treena said.

"What?"

"Oh, did I say that out loud? Probably has long hairs poking out of her areolas. Areolas. I like that word, say it with me Jess, come on – give me an A, give me an R, give me an E, give me an O- L - A. Areo…"

Jessica clasped her hand over her friend's mouth and looked around at the crowd.

"Shut up you fool; people are staring!"

"Oh, come on, lighten up. I can cheer just as well as her, and I don't even have humongous hooters!" Treena turned a serious face towards Jessica. "You're better than her. You know that, don't you?"

"Better than who? What are you talking about?"

"That bimbo you're staring at. The one with the hairy areolas! Like you're not thinking the same thing. And if you're worried about her getting her stuff all up in Derrick's face, well, I know Derrick would rather be with you, but if you don't make your move soon, I don't know — she's got some jugs on her that he may just want to get a hold of. Even if they are hairy," she giggled.

"Would you stop it! Derrick wouldn't stoop that low," Jessica said, taking another sip. Feeling a warm flush rise from her stomach up to her neck and face she continued. "Besides, I like Jack," she said with a smile, handing the flask back to Treena.

"That's my girl! Ya think you can score any booze for tomorrow's party?"

"Um, maybe some Mogen David."

"Seriously! Isn't that the stuff you Catholics drink at church? Don't your folks have anything stronger, like, you know, Johnny, Jim, Jose, or even your new friend, Jack?"

"I have no idea who all you are talking about," Jessica giggled.

"Oh wow, girl, you have a lot to learn."

Hmm, RB considered what she was hearing. *Not so sure I care much for this Treena chick, although some funny stuff does fall out of her mouth on occasion. Still, not sure I like the path she is trying to lead Jessica down.*

***

Arriving home from Saturday morning practice, Derrick walked into the house to the rich smell of coffee and muffins permeating the air. Having seen Darnell's truck in the driveway, he wasn't surprised to see him sitting at the kitchen table buttering a steaming blueberry muffin.

"Hey, Der," Darnell said with a big grin as he lifted a muffin to his mouth, bits of it falling off and scattering in his beard. "You were awesome in the scrimmage last night! Why didn't you tell me you were going to be the quarterback?"

"Aw, no big deal. Second string, probably won't get any real playing time."

"Well, if the way you played during that scrimmage is any indication, I think coach will be moving you to first string perty soon."

Derrick picked up a kitchen chair and swung it around, sitting in it backward, his hands resting on the top. His mother walked by and tousled his hair. "You were pretty amazing, son," she said, reaching in the cabinet and getting a plate. "You want some milk with your muffins?"

"Yeah, Ma, thanks," Derrick said, standing up and walking to the sink to wash his hands.

"Didn't you guys get enough soap last night to wash up with after practice?" his mother chided.

Derrick grinned. "Look at me, Ma, does it look like I cleaned up before I came home?"

Emma peered over her glasses at Derrick. "Guess not," she said, putting two muffins on the plate and setting them at the table along with a glass of milk.

"Hey, Der, I'm heading to Des Moines tomorrow to look at a tractor. How about making the drive with me? I could use the company," Darnell asked Derrick while lifting his coffee cup to his mouth.

"Oh, man, I can't. I promised Jessica I'd help her study for a world history test we're having on Monday. Sorry, bro, next time, ok?" Derrick said, sitting down at the table across from Darnell and taking a big bite of muffin. He hated turning down Darnell, but he really wanted to see Jessica. He recalled scanning the crowd during the football game and looking for her every chance he got.

Darnell raised an eyebrow and looked at his little brother. "My, my, I was wondering when you two would realize you weren't brother and sister," he chuckled.

Derrick took a big slug of milk while trying to think of a response. He never was good at pulling the wool over Darnell's eyes.

"Yeah, well, we're still just friends, but I was kinda hoping," he bent down over the table towards Darnell and lowered his voice hoping his mother wouldn't hear, "that, ya know, she might want to, I don't know, be more than friends. There's this party tonight at Collin's house, and I'm pretty sure she'll be there."

"Well, make your move, big guy. You already know she likes you."

"Yeah, likes me like a brother." Derrick looked over his shoulder at his mother who was busy washing dishes. "Let's go outside," he whispered conspiratorially.

Darnell grinned. He wondered when little bro' was going to start noticing girls.

Oh happy, happy, joy, joy! RB exclaimed. *I hope big brother can help Derrick get the ball rolling! I do love to see young love blossom, but I'm curious how Missy is doing this morning,* RB thought, lifting her cups and heading to Missy's home.

"Thanks for the muffins, Mom," Darnell said, bringing his dishes to the sink and giving his mother a light peck on the cheek. "I need to get home and start on my honey-do list." "Derrick, walk me to my truck?"

"Yeah, sure." Derrick quickly scooted his chair back causing it to tip. Swiftly, he grabbed the top of the chair before it toppled over.

Emma smiled to herself. *I may be getting old,* she thought, *but I'm not deaf.* She hoped Darnell could give her youngest some sound advice. She worried about Derrick. He had always been the perfect son. Too perfect. He needed to kick up his heels a little and have some fun. He didn't need to spend all his time studying or helping on

114

the farm. She was incredibly happy when Charles agreed to let him play football. He was much more relaxed with Derrick than he had been with the older boys. Sometimes she wondered if he regretted not allowing his other sons to participate in sports. Charles had worked the ground since he was old enough to plant a seed, and the farm was his legacy. One he intended to pass on to his children. Her face softened thinking of her son, Tim, who at the tender age of eighteen had decided farm life was not for him. One spring morning instead of getting on the tractor, he hopped in his car with his girlfriend, Julia, and headed west. Oh, how they fretted over him. She sighed, drained the water from the sink and walked to the kitchen table and sat down heavily. The past is the past, she thought. Tim had made a life for himself in California. He and Julia were married in Las Vegas and began a family of their own. It saddened her to recall she wasn't asked to attend their wedding, but she was also grateful their boys, her grandsons, Jerry and James, came and stayed on the farm with them for a week just about every summer when they were growing up. At least until high school when summer jobs and girlfriends took the place of going to Grandma Em's. Taking the red-checkered gingham dishcloth off her shoulder, she dried her hands and smiled thinking about last Thanksgiving. She had so much to be thankful for. All her children and grandchildren had come home. She couldn't remember when they had last all been together. Jerry had gotten so tall. He was attending college at UCLA and was a joy to visit with, although she did wish he would at least trim his long black hair. She couldn't help but chuckle when she thought of his hair. With his dark-rimmed glasses and his hair pulled back in a ponytail he looked like a bohemian. Her chuckle turned into a grin as she reminisced about their talk which lasted until the wee hours of the morning. *I may have told him too much,* Emma thought, her cheeks beginning to show a faint blush recalling telling him about her younger years when she was a bit of a rebel. *He would have fit right in with my era,* she thought before switching to thoughts of his brother, James. He was in his last year of high school, and Derrick was enthralled with his talks of the big city. Emma was fearful James would plant seeds in Derrick which would grow to the point that he, like his brother, Tim, would someday want to establish his life away from the farm. She smiled. She knew she needn't worry. She knew Derrick enjoyed his life in Iowa, and perhaps Charles had relaxed his farming demands on Derrick so he wouldn't rebel and escape to parts unknown the way Tim did.

***

Darnell and Derrick walked towards Darnell's Ram truck. Lightly punching Derrick in the arm, Darnell said with a grin, "So, what's up with Jessica? She sure has turned into one perty filly."

Derrick stopped walking and looked at the ground and kicked at a dirt clod. Feeling his cheeks start to burn, he wondered how to tell Darnell that Jessica was more than 'perty'. She was totally beautiful, and she made him feel things he didn't know how to deal with. How could he tell his brother that when he looked at her, he found it hard to look at her face and that his eyes always headed to her breasts? How could he tell him he wanted to pull her close and kiss her when he had never kissed a girl before and had no clue how to go about it? How could he admit to Darnell that if he didn't halt his thoughts of her, he knew they would go places which would force him to go to confession and do a gazillion Hail Mary's. *Were thoughts sins?* he wondered. He looked up at his brother, his foot still kicking at the ground causing little puffs of dust to float around their ankles.

"Oh, nothing. Mr. Johnson said we should study together when he caught me giving her an answer in history class."

"And...," Darnell said, raising an eyebrow and assessing Derrick. He noted the flushed cheeks and the lack of eye contact. *He has it bad,* Darnell thought. *I sure was lucky with Elaine. It's a good thing she asked me to the Sadie Hawkins dance, or I'd probably still be single.* He smiled to himself remembering their early courtship days.

Shrugging his shoulders, Derrick did not respond.

Throwing his arm over Derrick's shoulder, Darnell pulled him close and gave him a nuggie.

"Ow!" Derrick yelped, pulling away and rubbing his head. "I don't know why I thought I could talk to you anyway."

"Hey, come on, you get harder knocks than that on the football field. I'm sorry, it's just, well, geez, it's been a long time since I dated and well, Elaine always sort of took the lead. Good thing she did 'cuz I don't know how I ever would have worked up the nerve to ask her first."

"Really?" Derrick said, lowering his hands and slipping them into his pockets. It never occurred to him that Darnell was ever shy around girls.

"Just relax and be yourself. You two are like peas in a pod. You already know she likes you. The real you, and that's important. Maybe, I don't know, touch her hand when you're studying, tell her she looks nice, but be subtle. She'll get the hint. Just let nature take its course," Darnell said with a wink as he opened the door to his truck. "Oh, and when she talks, listen," he grinned. "Women like it when they think you're listening to them. You'll be fine," Darnell said, jumping into his truck.

Derrick watched his brother drive off, dust spewing out a trail behind him. Darnell stuck his arm out the window and gave a wave and a thumbs up.

Just be myself, yeah, that's really getting me somewhere, Derrick thought, trodding back to the house. Taking the steps to the porch two at a time he sat down in one of the rockers. Bruiser, who had been napping in a sunbeam by the side of the chair, opened his eyes and looked at Derrick. His tail began thumping against the wooden floor of the porch. Reaching down, Derrick scratched the old dog's ears.

THE RED BRA

***

RB arrived just as Missy woke up. She watched Missy roll over and grab her phone from the bedside table. 11:32 glared at her in bold red letters. She laid her phone down and grabbed the spare pillow lying by her side. Hugging it close to her chest, she smiled. She was so nervous when she ran out to the football field with her squad that she thought she was going to either puke, pass out, or both. It was all she could do to keep the smile Coach insisted was always present plastered on her face. However, once they began their routine, the crowd faded into a blur, and she lost herself in the rhythm of her movements. Ever since she was a little girl, she loved to dance. Cheering gave her the same feeling as dancing did. She liked being in the spotlight. She rolled over on her side and scrunched her legs up, savoring the memories of her first time cheering before a crowd.

"Ow!" she yelled as her breasts fell together with her movement. *Geez,* she thought, *why are my titties so sore?* She put her hands to her breasts and gently massaged them through the oversized t-shirt she wore as a nightgown. *My god, they hurt! I'm not due for my period for what, another two weeks. Why the heck are they so sore? Oh, duh…. all that jumping up and down in my el cheapo Wally World bra.* Missy rolled over on her back and stared at the ceiling. *I hate being so dang poor. Thank god Carolyn's parents paid for all my cheer-leading expenses. At least I think they did. Someone did.*

All she knew was when she made the squad coach gave her two uniforms and a sweat suit and said they had already been paid for. She knew darn good and well Christy wouldn't have forked over the bucks. She thought back to when she told her mom she was trying out for the squad. All her mother did was tell her by god she wasn't paying for any of those cheerin' clothes and she better up her babysitting gigs if she expected to have the dough to pay for those fancy dancy outfits. Missy cringed at the memories of that day. The only people she ever babysat for were a few of her mom's clients at the beauty salon. She had put a sign in the shop where her mom worked offering her services. She surprised herself at how much she enjoyed her little charges. Even little Timmy, who loudly proclaimed, 'I'm gonna put on my cowboy boots and kick you!' as soon as his parents left for an evening of sushi. She laughed out loud at the memory. She recalled that as soon as he put cowboy boots on his little five-year-old feet and came stomping up to her, she got down on all fours and said, 'Come on little doggie, get on your horse and ride!' They had been best buds ever since. Dianna, his mother, told her he frequently begged them to go have 'shush he' so she could come over and play horsey.

Sitting up, Missy stretched her hands up over her head. *Man, my boobs **really** hurt.* She looked down at her chest. *I'm not sure inheriting Grandma's assets was the best thing for me.* Getting up, she walked over to her dresser. Opening her sock drawer, she dug to the back and pulled out a pair of thick black socks she had stuffed in the back.

Unrolling the socks, she laid out the bills she had hidden in them. *Thirty-six dollars. Surely that's enough to buy a decent bra.*

Seriously! I mean really, girl! With what you got going on, you're gonna need some serious support! RB exclaimed, pushing out her cups and straightening her straps. *I know it's been a while since I left the shelf, and I know I'm, well, ahh, let's say, I'm of a premium caliber, but lord knows even bras a few steps below me are gonna cost a bit more than thirty-six dollars! How can you not know that?*

Missy stuffed the bills back into the sock and closed her drawer. Strolling into the kitchen, she opened the refrigerator and stared at the contents. Beer on the bottom shelf, pickles and mayo in the door, a container of something left over from a restaurant her mother must have gone to last night resting by itself on the middle shelf. She picked up the container and opened it. "Phew," she said out loud, waving her hand across her face. *I hope that tasted better than it smells,* she thought, closing the refrigerator door and grabbing what was left of a loaf of bread off the top of the refrigerator, hoping there would be something besides heels to toast. As she popped the bread into the toaster, she heard her mother walk into the kitchen. *For being a beautician, her hair sure looks like crap most of the time,* Missy thought, watching her mother walk past her and head to the coffee pot without uttering a word. Missy stood silently in front of the toaster willing it to pop before her mother spoke, so she could grab her toast and retreat to her room. The disappointment of her mother not showing up for her first cheerleading gig still hung heavy on her heart. She knew deep inside she wouldn't come, but it didn't stop the little girl inside her from wanting her mother to be in the crowd, beaming with pride at her only child, her daughter, who had busted her butt to win a spot on the squad.

"Throw a few in for me," Christy muttered when Missy's toast popped up. Missy pulled her toast from the toaster and inserted two fresh slices. She glanced over at her mother who stood staring at the coffee pot, no doubt willing it to perk faster. The silence reined heavy as the two stood, waiting for bread to toast and coffee to perk.

By the looks of it, Mom must have tied one on again last night, Missy thought while buttering her toast. Christy's short hair stuck out in different directions; the bleach blond ends glaring in stark contrast to the brown roots. She was wearing a tight pair of low-cut short shorts with a loose-fitting V-neck top. Reaching for the top shelf of the cabinet for powdered creamer her shirt raised, exposing the tattoo of a butterfly surrounded by colorful swirls across her lower back. Missy averted her eyes from her mother's backside, only to glance down her mother's thin legs where her eyes rested on the chain of butterflies surrounding her left ankle. She was barefoot, and her brightly polished pink toenails reflected the single beam of sunlight streaming through the crack in the curtains. The dust motes playfully danced as they followed the stream of light on its way down to her feet.

Whoa, RB thought while checking out Christy, *I was feeling kinda bad for Missy since her mom didn't show up to watch her cheer, but on second thought, ewww! I think she's better off not letting too many people know she's her mama!*

Missy thought back to her younger years when she would sit next to her mother as she lounged on the couch watching her soaps. Scrunching herself between the end of the couch and her mother's bare feet, she would try to count the butterflies; her tiny fingers hovering over each one as she marveled at the bright colors. She flinched remembering being kicked when her counting efforts annoyed her mother. *No wonder I hate butterflies,* she thought, watching her mother lean on the counter, her shirt gaping and exposing yet another butterfly perched on the curve of her partially exposed breast. *No wonder I flunked kindergarten too,* she grimly thought. Her memories of the first year in kindergarten were dim, but she remembered enough to now wonder why her mother never showed her how to hold a pencil or sing the ABC's before sending her off to a place where everyone else could write their name and count to ten.

Missy carried her toast back to her room, leaving her mother to continue to stare zombie-like at the coffee pot. Sitting down at her desk, she pulled her iPad out from

123

under a pile of textbooks. She smiled, running her index finger over the picture of Grandma Lila that was taped to the top. Her grandma had given her the iPad for her sixteenth birthday. She sure missed her since she moved to Michigan to live with her Aunt Betsy. Every time she sent a gift she always taped a picture of herself to it. Missy's mother said it was to rub it in her face that she couldn't afford to buy lavish gifts for her daughter. Missy knew it was just her way of trying to be near her. They had a bond miles could not erase. Missy sighed, *I miss her so much,* she thought, opening her iPad and googling bras. Her mouth dropped open when she saw the vast array of bras available - and the prices. "Good lord," she said out loud, clicking on an ad that proclaimed, *'wide bra selection',* inwardly wondering if that meant for women with wide boobs or if they had a lot of different bras. She clicked on the picture of a lacy purple bra that stated it was a seamless full figure wire bra. *What the heck's a wire bra?* she muttered to herself, enlarging the picture. *Well, it got five stars in the rating reviews, so that's good. Oh, my god! Sixty-five dollars? You have got to be kidding me,* she thought, reading the price. *That thing must be spun from gold or at least silver plated. Hmm, provides terrific uplift, great for sagging.* She looked down at her girls. *You don't sag. At least I have that going for me,* she thought, recalling how her Grandma's boobs appeared to touch her navel when she saw her in her nightgown. *Wonder what else these over the shoulder boulder holders do besides be uplifting,* she thought, continuing to read through the bra's attributes. "Oh, mercy," she giggled out loud and then giggled even louder when she realized she had uttered one of Grandma's favorite euphemisms. *They even smooth out back fat!* Sitting back, she stared at the screen shaking her head. *I definitely don't have back fat.*

Awesome! RB exclaimed, coming in closer to get a better view of her sister bras.

Missy returned to the search engine and typed in underwire bra. Clicking on Wikipedia, she discovered that underwire bras have been around since 1893. *Hmm, why haven't I ever heard of these things?* she thought, continuing to read. *So, they lift, shape, and support. Support, that's what I need. Oh, my, they've been known to set off metal detectors and deflect bullets! Well, fat chance of me ever getting on a plane, and I don't think the crime rate is high enough around here for me to worry about deflecting bullets, but hey, I'm thinking one of these underwire things might make me sort of like wonder woman. Or would that be Superman, what with deflecting bullets and all,* she thought wryly. *Okay, I guess what I need is an underwire bra. I wonder if Grandma knows about these?*
Hitting the back button, she clicked on an ad for underwire bras.
Alright, this is more like it. Fourteen-fifty for an underwire bra. She clicked on the picture of a black bra

that said it was the 'ultimate' and scrolled down to the reviews. *Oh, wow, Ms 38DD says it's a great bra.*

RB perked up hearing the words double D.

Missy scribbled down the brand name, folded the paper in half, and shoved it in her purse. *Now, to get Carolyn to give me a ride to the mall before our next game,* she thought, closing her iPad.

Oh, what fun! I do hope Carolyn is well versed in the many styles available, and of course, steers her away from those knock-off knocker versions! RB exclaimed before sailing off to check on Jessica.

***

Jessica woke up Saturday morning to the sound of her mother vacuuming. *Oh lordy,* she grimly thought, *why does she have to clean so early on the only day I get to sleep in?* She threw her pillow over her head to muffle the sounds outside her bedroom door. Unable to fall back to sleep, she reflected on the football scrimmage the night before. Treena wanted her to go riding around after the game, but she had promised her mother she would come home as soon as it was over. She for sure didn't want to risk getting grounded and miss the party at Collin's. Collin's father was some hot shot executive, and they had a gigantic home on the edge of town. His father was frequently out of town on business, and his mother let him have friends over pretty much anytime he wanted. They had a huge basement with a pool table on one end, and a seventy-inch flat screen TV covered the wall on the other. She had never been to any of his parties, but she had heard all about the house from her mother, who had once been on the local fair committee with his mother, and the meetings were held there. She remembered her mother going on and on to her father about the lovely pool, the outdoor kitchen, and the rose garden.

Jessica rolled out of bed and stood in front of her mirror. *Oh, great, another zit.* Leaning in closer to examine a white pustule that had grown overnight in the crease by her nose. She leaned in closer and squeezed the pimple; leaving a small, red, oozing open sore in its place. *Oh, that was smart, retard,* she said to herself, heading towards the bathroom in search of Clearasil to dab on her now bleeding crater. Locating the zit cream from the bottom drawer of the bathroom vanity, Jessica's head began to swim when she stood. Quickly, she grabbed the edge of the sink until she regained her balance. *Holy Crap,* she thought to herself. *What the heck was that all about!* Slowly, she walked into the kitchen and poured herself a large glass of milk. Her tongue felt oddly strange as she guzzled the milk, attempting to quench her thirst and diminish the fuzzy feeling on her tongue and the rumbling in her stomach. *I wonder if Jack did this to my mouth?* she thought, setting the empty glass on the counter and reaching in the cabinet for a pop-tart. Turning from the cabinet, she began to unwrap the tart when her younger sister, Darci, walked in and sat down at the table. She grabbed a banana from the fruit bowl on the table and stared at her sister.

"What are you staring at?" Jessica curtly asked her sister as she took a bite of pop-tart.

"What's that mess on your nose? You get in a fight or something?"

"Shut-up," Jessica said, self-consciously lifting her finger to the crevice between her nose and cheek. She looked at her moist finger; dabs of white cream mixed with flecks of blood now covering its tip.

"Eww, that's gross. It's a pimple, isn't it? Mom says you're not supposed to pick pimples, so does Miss Moore. She says to leave blackheads alone too. She says they'll get infected. She says if you wash your face every day and eat right you won't get them," Darci said, waving her banana in the air before pointing it at Jessica's pop tart.

"Well, monkeys eat bananas, and you look like a monkey," Jessica shot back, glaring at her sister.

Putting her free hand under her armpit, Darci began saying, "*ah ah ah, ooh ooh ooh*" while bits of banana fell from her mouth.

Jessica couldn't help but grin at her sister's monkey imitation. "You are one lame monkey," she said, sitting down next to Darci. "Is it *that* bad?"

"Naw, not since you wiped all that goop off."

Jessica looked at her hand and self-consciously wiped the remnants of goo on her pajama bottoms. "You just wait," she teased her sister, "it won't be long before you wake up to a pizza face staring at you in the mirror."

"Not gonna happen," she replied, removing the remaining peel from her banana and dropping it on the table. "I wash my face every day, and I eat healthy," she said, pointing the remaining bite of banana at her sister before popping it into her mouth.

RB shimmied her cups and straps in delight, relishing the banter between the sisters.

The sounds of vacuuming ceased and their mother, Meredith, walked into the kitchen. "How are my two favorite girls doing this morning?" She smiled, walking to the coffee pot and pouring herself a fresh cup. "I didn't hear you girls get up. I was going to make French toast for breakfast," she said, eyeing the banana peel on the table and the pop-tart that was making the journey to its final destination in Jessica's mouth.

"French toast is full of carbs and sugar and stuff," Darci said. "Miss Moore says you should start your day off with protein and fruit. I'll have some scrambled eggs."

Meredith raised an eyebrow at her youngest. "Please, Mom would you cook me some scrambled eggs? Or have you not yet reached the chapter in health class on manners?"

"Please, Mom, would you please fix me some scrambled eggs, please?" Darci batted her eyes at her mother. "Please."

Meredith looked at her youngest daughter and shook her head. "Since you asked so nicely, yes, I would be more than happy to fix you some eggs. How about you Jess, you up for some eggs? Lord knows we have enough! Those hens have sure been prolific lately. Oh, Jess, do you think you could take some eggs down to the Murphy's sometime today? I saw Emma in the store yesterday, and she had eggs in her cart. I didn't realize they quit raising chickens. Don't know why she didn't ask us for some. I told her we had plenty and insisted she take a few dozen off our hands."

RB perked up, *Oh the gods are with you, Jess! Say yes, say yes!*

Hearing her mother mention the Murphy's, Jessica's heart skipped a beat. Raising her finger, she gently touched the spot by her nose. It was starting to crust over as the blood spot dried. *I don't think there's enough make-up in the universe to cover this zit,* she thought, wondering what time Derrick got home from football practice.

"Der's coming over to help me study for our world history test tomorrow. Maybe he could take them then, or you could hand em off at church?" She wasn't sure she wanted him to see her looking like Rudolph the red nosed reindeer as she was convinced by now her entire nose was becoming red and turning into one ginormous zit.

"I really need you to deliver them today, hon. They probably will want eggs for breakfast before church. Now, do you want eggs or not?" she said, cracking eggs in a bowl for Darci.

"I thought French toast sounded good," she said, grinning mischievously at her sister who promptly stuck her tongue out.

"On top of a pop-tart? I'll have to agree with Miss Moore on this one. I think a little protein would be better," she said, removing two more eggs from the carton and cracking them into the bowl.

Darci sat up straight and started to speak, but Jessica's glare stopped her.

Meredith glanced back and forth at her daughters. "What's going on between you two?" she queried, pouring the eggs in the skillet.

"Nothing," they said in unison, as the fake smiles they shot towards their mother belied the prior barbs they had been tossing back and forth.

"How was the scrimmage last night, Jessica?" her mother asked, setting the steaming scrambled eggs in front of her daughters. "You shot into your room so fast we didn't get a chance to chat."

"Oh, it was alright. I was just tired."

"Bet you didn't wash your face. That's why you got that big ol' zit." Darci couldn't help but give one more dig at her sister. *Her perfect sister who never did anything wrong*, she thought to herself, secretly hoping her whole face would turn into one big fat zit. *That way, when she popped it her brains would explode, and she could quit hearing everyone brag about how smart and perfect she was.*

"Mom!" Jessica whined, her voice imploring her mother to make her sister shut up.

"That will be quite enough, Darci. Now finish up your eggs and get off your duff and help me clean up this kitchen."

"How come Jessica doesn't have to help clean? She never has to do anything," Darci sat back in her chair and crossed her arms, shooting daggers at her sister.

Jessica finished her eggs and guzzled her second glass of milk, glad the queasiness in her stomach was beginning to cease while ignoring the barbs her sister was shooting at her with her eyes.

"Because Jessica has to deliver eggs. Now Jessica, make sure you get the ones from the back of the fridge. I want the Murphy's to have the freshest ones."

"Can I at least take a shower first?"

Meredith glanced at the clock. "I suppose, but make it quick. I need some help around the house today, and please check on the goats. That little rascal, Juniper, has been gnawing on the fence. Rub some bitter apple on it. Dad doesn't have time to rebuild fences."

Jessica hurried through her shower being careful not to scrub her face too harshly. Gently, she applied concealer and was relieved to note the pimple barely showed. She threw on a pair of jeans and thumbed through the shirts in her closet trying to decide what to wear. *Oh, geez,* she

132

thought, vetoing one shirt after another. *It's just Derrick. I'm delivering eggs for crying out loud. Like he would even notice what I'm wearing. That is if he's even home from practice yet.* She grabbed a blue Lincoln High shirt which proudly proclaimed, *Home of the Wildcats.*

Oh, come on already! RB implored, unheard. *Don't you realize the way you look is only important the first time you meet? You two are so beyond that! He sees the real you, just like you see the real Derrick.*

Walking towards the side door that led to the garage, Jessica grabbed her mother's keys from the counter. "Ma, I'm going," she shouted, plucking her jacket from one of the hooks which ran the length of the small entryway by the back door.

"Don't forget, get the freshest eggs!" her mother shouted from the kitchen.

"Got it," Jessica said, walking down the few steps into the garage and over to the ancient refrigerator nestled between her dad's workbench and bins of her mother's hobby supplies. "Good lord," Jessica mumbled, surveying the massive amount of eggs in the refrigerator. Reaching towards the back, she grabbed three cartons and held them carefully while using her hip to close the door.

Hopping in her mother's Camry, she drove the short distance down the road to Derrick's. Butterflies swirled in her stomach as she neared his drive. *What is wrong with me,* she thought. *It's just Derrick.* Pulling into the drive, she immediately saw Derrick sitting on the front porch petting Bruiser. Smiling, she remembered the day Bruiser came to live with Derrick. *Gosh, what were we, seven or eight years old? We had been down by the pond behind his house trying to catch crawdads. I had my sand bucket, and Derrick had a big ol' five-gallon bucket he had absconded from the barn. We were furiously digging at the chimney-like tubes protruding helter-skelter from the ground like an industrial park that had gone defunct when a dog appeared, seemingly out of nowhere.* She recalled seeing a bedraggled pup sitting on the other side of the pond, his head cocked sideways, watching them. When he saw Jessica looking at him, he stood up and began furiously wagging his tail. Her smile widened at the memory, and she remembered how he flopped down and bared his belly when they walked over to him. His hair was matted and covered with cockleburs. Derrick tenderly picked him up and held him in his arms like a baby while Jessica carefully tried to remove the burrs, pricking her fingers in the process. She remembered Derrick looking at the spots of blood on her fingers caused by the burrs and asking her to hold the now wiggling puppy while he had a go at the burrs. *He was even looking out for me way back then,* Jessica thought, stopping the car and picking up the eggs. Bruiser's ears perked up at the sound of the car door closing, and he scrambled off the porch to greet her. "Hey, ol' buddy, how the heck ya' doin'?" Jessica crooned to the dog while scratching behind his ears. His entire body wiggled with delight, and he made small yowling sounds in his excitement at seeing her.

Derrick stood up and hopped down the steps two at a time. "I think someone misses you," he grinned. "I think that sound is dog speak for I love you." Derrick stopped in his tracks. *Oh, crap, what did I just say?* he thought to himself. Before he could continue to berate himself further, Jessica squatted and placed the egg cartons on the ground. Bruiser promptly laid down and rolled over with all fours in the air begging for a tummy rub. Jessica obliged by furiously rubbing his belly and proclaiming her mutual love for him.

Earth to Jessica! RB shouted unheard. *Did you not just hear that Freudian slip? Good grief,* RB shook herself back and forth.

"Gotta love this mutt, huh Der? I am so glad no one claimed him, and your folks let you keep him."

"Yeah," Derrick grinned, the blush receding from his face, realizing Jessica didn't read anything more into his 'love you' faux pas. "Remember all those flyers we made to post around town to try and find his owner?"

"Yeah," she smiled at the memory. "Didn't your folks say you could keep him if no one claimed him within a month?"

"Yeah, and do you remember where we posted those flyers?"

"Uh, nowhere?"

Derrick laughed. "I think we put a few in places where Ma might see them so that she knew we were trying."

"Well, he was meant to be yours. He sure has been a good dog, hasn't he?" Jessica said, scooping up the egg cartons and holding them out to Derrick. "Mom ran into your mother at the grocery store the other day. She about had a fit when she saw your mom with eggs in her cart. She told her not to buy any and sent me down with some. Seriously, please let me know when you're running low on eggs. Those chickens of Dad's don't know the meaning of lay off. Get it," she snickered, punching him lightly in the arm. "Lay off; chickens lay eggs."

"You are so lame," Derrick said with a snicker. "So, your mom didn't want my mom to put all her eggs in one basket?"

"Now who's the lame one?"

"That would be a duck, lame duck, get it."

She stuck her tongue out at him.

"Hey, what's good for the goose is good for the gander!"

"Enough already," Jessica said laughing, "or I'm gonna cook your goose!"

Derrick's grin widened.

"Well, I better get home. Mom needs me to put some sort of crap on the goats' pen. I guess Juniper's been chewing on the fence."

"Aww, he's probably just bored. Why don't you bring Bruiser home for a spell? I bet he could get old Juni's mind off fence chewing."

"And leave you unprotected, not a chance!"

"And just what do you think I need protection from?"

"Oh, I don't know, spiders? Centipedes?"

Derrick looked at her, confused for a second. Remembering, he laughed loudly. "Hey, I was what, five years old? How do you remember that stuff anyway?"

"Oh, you screaming like a girl left a definite impression on my brain," she said with a smile, recollecting the time they were moving old bricks from the side of the barn in search of treasure. She had used a stick to flick over a brick, and when she did, centipedes, spiders, and black crickets came charging out and began running haphazardly towards them.

"And if I recall," he said smiling, "you managed to get to the safety of the porch faster than I did."

"We never did find any treasure that year, did we?" her voice took on a serious note, her thoughts growing pensive reflecting on the carefree days of their childhood.

"Nah, but if you want, I bet Mom could dig out some of our old treasure maps, and we could keep looking."

"Who made those treasure maps anyway?"

"I think Elaine probably did. Remember when we found the first map? We really thought we found something big. X marks the spot!" He laughed. "Didn't we find some quarters or something one time?"

"Yeah, I think we did, and you wouldn't share because you said they were in your yard."

"Did I really? Geez, Jess, I'm sorry." Reaching into his pocket, he scrounged for a quarter. Pulling one out, he flicked it at her.

Ducking, she laughed as the quarter made its way towards her head. "That's okay. I think I found some quarters I never told you about."

"What! You've been holding out on me all these years!" Walking towards her, he picked up the quarter which lay at her feet. "I'm keepin' this," he chuckled. "Even, Steven?"

"Deal, Camille," she replied.

They stood grinning at each other, both caught up in the memories of their childhood antics.

Jessica turned and walked towards the car.

"Hey, we still on for tomorrow, you know, me helping you help me save trees?" Derrick asked, aware the tone of his voice sounded a little higher than he expected.

"Yeah, sure, but I'll see you at Collin's party tonight, won't I?"

"Oh yeah, for sure. See you later." Derrick gave a slight wave as Jessica got in the car and headed for home.

Derrick's grin filled his entire face as he walked to the house with Bruiser playfully nipping at his heels. Reaching down, he patted his buddy on the head. "I think she just may like me more than a bro', what do you think old pal?"

Bruiser wagged his tail, and Derrick took that as a yes.

Ahh, there's nothing much better than watching young love, except, of course, being the one in love, RB wistfully thought while taking to the sky to check on Missy's bra progress.

Chapter 10
Carolyn

Picking up her phone, Missy texted Carolyn.

u up

yeah

can i come over

k

Missy tied her hair back in a ponytail and grabbed a pair of jeans from the pile of clothes lying on the floor by her bed. She picked up the faded and worn bra she had tossed on her dresser the night before. She grimly looked at the bra; the sides threadbare and misshapen from being stretched so many times. *Hopefully,* she thought while wrapping the bra around her midsection and clasping it on the first hooks, *you will be headed for the trash bin by the time this day is over.* Missy finished dressing and grabbed her thirty-six dollars from the sock drawer. Hearing the shower running, she scribbled a quick note to her mother and stuck it on the refrigerator door.

Quickly, she walked the twenty-seven steps to the Browne's back door. She couldn't seem to walk over there without counting. It was a habit from her younger days when she and Carolyn first counted the steps so they could meet exactly half-way before heading to the park or to whatever adventure they had planned for the day. Missy's mood was light as she rapped on the door with her signature, shave and a hair-cut - two bits, knock.

Opening the door, Jeff smiled upon seeing Missy. "Hey, you were supposed to let me do the 'two bits'.

Missy returned his smile. "Didn't know you were right there, or I would have waited." She remembered the days when she and Carolyn would go out to his shed and knock on his door; tap – tap tap tap – tap. If he wasn't busy, he would tap – tap back, and they would go inside. He would lift them on to his workbench and talk to them while he made birdhouses or fixed broken toys. Missy used to secretly pretend he was her daddy. He was the one who taught them their secret knock.

"Carolyn's down in the basement. You know the way," he said, moving to the side allowing her to enter.

Missy scrambled down the steps taking them two at a time. She nearly fell when she hit the slick floor at the foot of the steps.

"Whoa, where's the fire?" Joan asked while Missy tried to maintain her balance.

"Sorry, guess I'm still a little hyped up from the game last night."

"I didn't get a chance to see you after the game. You looked wonderful! I was so proud of you. I know how hard you worked to get a spot on the squad."

Missy's grin filled her face when she looked at Joan. "Thanks, that means a lot to me. I was kinda nervous at first, but once we got going it was so much fun!"

"Well, it showed on your face! Carolyn's in the laundry room folding clothes. I'm sure she wouldn't mind some help folding the towels and whatnot."

"K, uh, nice to see you," Missy said, rounding the corner towards the laundry room. The Brownes had a spacious home with a full basement. Their laundry room was as big as Missy's living room and kitchen combined. Sometimes she wondered how a house as small and dull as theirs ended up in a neighborhood that was mostly big homes with fancy yards.

"Hey," Missy said, walking in and sitting down on one of the stools that stood by the counter lining the wall.

"Hey, yourself," Carolyn said, transferring clothes from the dryer to a basket. After removing all the dry clothes, she plopped the basket in front of Missy. As she began taking clothes out of the washer and placing them in the dryer, she glanced over her shoulder at Missy. "Make yourself useful and help me get these clothes folded. Once we're finished, we can decide what we're wearing to the party tonight."

"Yes, ma'am," Missy said, pulling a bath towel from the basket. "Why is it," she asked as she began folding a towel, "that I have no problem folding your family's laundry, but I hate folding laundry for my ma?"

"One of those weird universal laws, I guess. Like it's no fun to clean your own room, but kinda fun to clean someone else's."

"Let me get this straight, are you saying you want to have some fun and clean my room when we're done with the laundry?"

"Uh, nope, don't believe I said that at all," Carolyn looked over and grinned at her friend as she pulled a mesh bag from the washer and laid it on the counter beside Missy.

Missy looked at the bag. She could see it had bras in it.

"Soooo, you trap your bras in a bag, so they don't, what, mingle with the other unmentionables in there?"

Carolyn gave her a puzzled look. "How do you wash your bras?"

"Same way I wash everything else, just throw 'em in with whatever."

"Seriously? And they stay nice?"

Missy laughed, "My bras aren't exactly what you would call nice to begin with. That's why I came over, to see if you could take me bra shopping today. I got online, and did you know they make bras with wires under them to help, you know, keep the girls in place?"

Carolyn continued to stare at Missy with a puzzled look.

"Anyways," Missy continued, "my boobs are *killing* me from all that cheering. I mean, they were always a little sore after practicing and stuff, but I just thought that was my muscles getting a workout, but you know, I'm like, pretty in shape and stuff now, and when I got online and looked at bras... My god, I had no idea there were so many different kinds of bras!"

Carolyn wasn't sure how to respond. She knew Missy's mom didn't have much money, but it never occurred to her that Missy didn't at least have a decent bra.

Well, I don't know what to think! RB fluttered back and forth not sure what she felt as she realized just how much Missy didn't know about things most young ladies learned from their mothers at a much younger age than Missy was now.

"So," Carolyn said slowly, picking up the mesh bag and unzipping it. "What kind of bras have you been wearing?"

"Well, here," Missy began as she lifted her shirt, "you tell me."

Carolyn playfully put her hands over her eyes and turned her head. "Uh, no, that's okay, you probably have one similar to one of the ones in here," she said, beginning to take the clean bras out of the bag.

"You never said. Why do you put your bras in that bag to wash em?"

"So the hooks don't get caught on stuff, you know, and so the cups stay nice, and the straps don't get all wrapped up around your socks and things."

Missy laughed, "You mean all this time I didn't have to wangle my bras off the thingamajig in the middle of the washer or unhook 'em from my panties! Why doesn't my mom have one of them baggie things?"

"I don't know. Maybe her mom never used one, and she didn't know about them. Same as you."

Carolyn removed the bras from the bag and placed them in a row on the counter. "These are Mom's bras, so you may not have any like these." Reaching into the dryer, she pulled out another bag. "Some of mine are in here."

"*Some* of yours?" Missy asked incredulously. "How many bras do you have?"

"I don't know, seven or eight." She thought for a moment, "Well that's not counting the strapless bra I got for my cousin's wedding or my sport bras."

"Why do you have so many bras?"

"Same reason I have so many pairs of undies. I wear a fresh one every day, don't you?"

As soon as the words were out of Carolyn's mouth, she regretted them.

"I mean, well, I sweat a lot, and you know, they get cheesy. Geez, Missy, I'm sorry. I didn't mean anything by that. You never smell, honest."

Missy, shifting her eyes towards the ground before looking up at her friend replied, "No worries," and smiled while picking up one of Joan's bras. It was beige with a wide band in the back. The cups were slightly padded, and the straps were wider than what Missy had. "This looks like something my grandma would wear," she laughed. "Now this, ooh la la," she said, picking up a light blue bra covered with sheer lace. It had delicate satin straps and a thin band with single hooks.

"Shush," Carolyn said, looking towards the door, "do you want my mom coming in here and seeing us examining her bras?"

"Uh, no, but really, I mean your mom is *married*!"

"Yeah, it is a little creepy, huh? Here," she pushed her mother's bras to the side and unzipped the bag that held hers, "these are mine. This is the one I wore at last night's game."

"Oh yeah, I remember this one," Missy said, taking it from Carolyn's hand and turning the cup inside out.

"What are you doing?"

"Looking for used up band-aids."

Carolyn picked up a bra and threw it at her. "Hey, I took those off as soon as I got home."

"Bet that hurt."

"Nah, I use the ouchless ones, you know, the ones for little kids boo boo's."

Missy laughed, "Hey, you could market your own band-aids. You could call them Boob-Aids. Band-aids for boob-boobs!

Carolyn laughed along with her.

"Yeah," Missy continued, "we could market them by saying things like; When you're cold, are your nipples so hard they could cut glass? Do they embarrass you when they stand at attention for the entire world to see? Well, fear no more, Boob-Aids are here!"

"You really are a nut; you know that?"

"And proud of it!" Missy beamed, examining the bra Carolyn had tossed at her. "Yeah, this one is sorta like mine. It's thin like this. Lord knows I don't need any padding. Why don't you wear bras with padding?"

"Hey, I'm perfectly content with my size B," she giggled, starting to become a little embarrassed about all the breast talk.

"Do you have any with the wires?"

"No, I obviously don't need that kind of support," Carolyn said, looking down at her chest. "Here," she said, picking up one of her mother's bras. "This one has wires."

"Let me see," Missy said, reaching for the bra. "Ahh," she said, feeling the thin wire under the cups. "I can see how that would help. "Do you think you can drive me over to the mall today and help me pick out a couple? I have thirty-six dollars saved from babysitting, and online I saw where you could get some of these wired ones for like around fifteen dollars."

"Um, yeah, probably, I need to check with Mom. Now let's get this laundry finished so I can be on her good side before I ask."

Oh, goody, goody! Carolyn is going to help Missy get some bras! RB joyfully exclaimed, *And I can tell that young lady does have good taste in bras, even if they are a tad small.*

Ecstatic, Missy skipped across the yard to her home. She planned to offer to fix lunch for her mother before asking if she could go to the mall with Carolyn. She stopped skipping when she reached her driveway and realized her mother's car was gone. *Just as well,* she thought, walking into the house. *Hopefully, now I can leave with Carolyn before she gets home, and I won't have to risk her saying no.* Entering the kitchen, she saw her mother had scribbled a message on the back of her own note saying she got called into work, and Missy needed to dust and run the vacuum. *Okay,* Missy thought to herself, *weird that she still refuses to figure out texting, but I guess I'm glad she doesn't.* They communicated more in short notes than in spoken words these days, and that was fine by Missy. She began her chores cheerfully, anticipating finally having a bra that not only fit but was cute.

After Missy left, Carolyn walked into the living room and sat down on the couch next to her mother who was leafing through a magazine.

"Did you and Missy have a nice chat? I could hear you two giggling all the way up here. Wish I could have that much fun doing laundry." Closing her magazine, she turned and smiled at her daughter.

"Um, yeah, you know Missy, she pretty much always finds something to laugh about."

"Yes, she usually is pretty cheerful. She's such a resilient young lady. But you know, I do worry about her. Do you think she's that happy? I mean, not having a dad, and having so many different men come in and out of her mother's life all the time. I would think that would be a little confusing for her."

"She never really talks about it. I get the feeling she's pretty much ignored at home, but I think that suits her just fine."

Joan reached over and patted her daughter on the leg. "You know," she paused, gently squeezing her leg, "I'm proud of you for being her friend and helping her with her cheering. If it wasn't for you, I doubt if she would have tried out for the squad, and if she had, I seriously doubt she would have made it if not for you and your sister's help with learning the cheers."

Carolyn looked up at her mother and saw the sadness in her eyes that was always present whenever her sister was mentioned. Rebecca's death was something they didn't talk about. It was almost as if her parents were pretending she was still away at college and would come bouncing through the door again. She had noticed her parents paid more attention to Missy since Rebecca was gone which was a good thing for Missy.

Carolyn looked down at her hands and fiddled with the birthstone ring that adorned her right ring finger. "Yeah, but sometimes it's hard. She sorta has a, you know, a reputation."

Joan, raising an eyebrow, looked at her daughter.

"But, it's not true!" she quickly added. "At least I don't think it's true," she mumbled quietly. "I mean, I know she flirts a lot, and she, you know, wears clothes that, well, you see how she dresses. The other girls on the squad don't really like her."

"But do they know her?"

"That's the thing, Ma, they don't. They all think she's after their boyfriends or something."

"Well, you know, she hasn't exactly had a good role model which is why it's important you show her the proper way to behave around guys."

"Yeah, right, but it's kinda hard when she's always bouncing her, uh, stuff around. That's sorta what I wanted to talk to you about."

They sat in silence for a few minutes. Carolyn continued to twirl her ring trying to decide how to begin.

"So," Joan began, "what is it you wanted to talk about?"

"Um, well can I drive Missy over to the mall today?"

Joan studied Carolyn's face. "Ok, what's going on? It's not like you to act shy about going to the mall."

"Mom, you have to promise you won't let Missy know I talked to you about this, okay? Promise?"

Joan's forehead furrowed. "As long as no laws are being broken, I promise."

"Well, you know, Missy was helping me with the laundry, and uh, well, she saw all our bras. Anyway, she started talking about how much her boo...I mean, breasts, hurt when she cheered. Mom, I think she only owns one bra! By the way she talked, I think it's just a flimsy stretched out thing that you know, doesn't give her any support. Then she said she had some money saved up from babysitting, and she wants me to take her bra shopping. But Ma, she only has thirty-six dollars, and she thinks she can buy two decent bras with that."

THE RED BRA

"Oh, my, the poor thing. I know her mother doesn't make much money, but I never dreamed she didn't at least buy her daughter a few decent bras. Especially since she is so, well, you know, advanced in that department."

"Yeah, and well, she may be able to get one decent bra with the money she has, that is, if it's on sale. Ma, you should have seen her face when she saw how many bras we had in the wash! What am I gonna do?"

Joan thought for a moment. "I tell you what. Take my Macy's card. I think I have some coupons too. Take her to the Macy's bra department. They have ladies there that will measure her and tell her exactly what size she needs. I have a feeling she probably has no real idea what she should be wearing. Now, I imagine the saleslady will show her bras that would be best for her, uh, build."

"But, ma," Carolyn interrupted, "she can't afford those bras."

"Hush, let me finish. Have her pick out two or three based on comfort and support. Well, the saleslady will probably do that anyway. If she starts to fuss about the price, tell her to try them on to get a feel for what kind of fit she needs. Then, I don't know, somehow tell her you have my Macy's charge card and if you use the card, you get an extra discount. By the way, you really do. Tell her if the price goes over she can pay me back a little at a time when she gets more babysitting money."

"But Mom," Carolyn implored, "she will know I said something to you!"

"Not if you play it right. Get yourself something too, that way you can say I will think the amount on the card is for whatever it is you buy."

Carolyn grabbed her mother and hugged her. "Mom, you're the best."

Wow, RB whispered to herself, *that mom absolutely is the best! I wonder if they will find any bras as lovely as me?*

***

Missy arrived home from the mall thrilled with her purchases. Happy her mother wasn't home yet; she walked to her bedroom clutching her package close to her chest. After removing the bras from the bag, she grabbed a pair of scissors from her desk. Carefully, she cut the tags off and slowly ran her fingers along the silky straps. She had no idea there were so many different bras available. She laid the bras on her bed. She couldn't believe her luck. They were on sale, buy one get one half price, plus, Carolyn let her use her charge card, and she got an even bigger discount. *She sure is a good friend,* Missy thought, pulling off her top and removing her faded, stretched out bra. She commenced to toss it in the trash, but just as she was about to drop it on top of used tissues and waded up papers, she stopped. She put the bra in the laundry basket in her closet. *Who knows,* she thought, *I might need it someday. Or maybe I can sell it at a yard sale. Can you sell something at a yard sale you bought at a yard sale?* she wondered thinking back to the bras her mother would periodically pick up for her at Good Will or yard sales during her growth spurt. She always said there was no sense in buying something new if you could get it used. It never bothered Missy because that's the way it had always been although now since she was older, she did notice her mother's clothes were frequently new.

Interesting, RB thought when she saw Missy toss her ratty bra into the dirty clothes pile. *I guess when you have never had much it's hard to let go. But girl, get out those new brassieres! I can't wait to see them!*

She couldn't believe she actually had four brand new bras. She wouldn't have to go in the bathroom stall to change clothes in PE class ever again. Picking up a beige one, she ran her fingers along the wires on the bottom. The lady who sized her was so nice. She smiled, thinking about the older women who measured her. She was a bit surprised that she didn't have to be topless to get measured. The lady seemed as happy as she did when she checked on her in the dressing room. Missy couldn't believe how great it felt to have a bra that didn't cut into her skin. She had no idea bras could be so comfortable. *Hmm, which one should I wear to the party tonight? I think the black one. Carolyn said I needed a black one to wear under my dark blouses. How come I never knew that?* She reached in the closet and picked out a black blouse with a deep V-neck and three-quarter length sleeves. *This will be perfect,* she thought, putting on her new bra and adjusting the girls. She stood in front of the mirror and admired her new figure before putting on her blouse. A wide grin spread across her face, anticipating a fun night, and a future of pain-free cheering.

Oh, man! RB whined. *I wanted to see all her new bras! I can't believe I missed the shopping trip! Where was I anyway? I swear, sometimes I feel like I'm in a time warp. I wonder if she bought a gorgeous red bra like me?*

Chapter 11
Party-time

Treena pulled up to Jessica's house a little before seven. When Jessica hopped in the car, Treena turned to her.

"Did you score any booze?"

"Huh, what?"

"You know, you were supposed to raid your parents' liquor stash."

"I told you, they only have church wine."

"Well, it's better than nothing, duh."

"Yeah, well, Darci was stuck to me like glue. Every time I got near the liquor cabinet, she appeared out of nowhere. Besides, they don't keep much around. I don't think I could have taken any without them noticing. Anyways, I don't plan on drinking."

"Yeah, right. Well," Treena pointed to her oversized purse on the floor by Jessica's feet. "when you change your mind, Phil got me vodka. Vodka's the way to go. Your folks can't smell it."

"Okay, and who's Phil?"

"Oh, you've probably seen him around. Tall guy, glasses, kind of skinny. He lives down the block from me. He works at the mini-mart on Broadway."

"So, I'm guessing he's twenty-one?"

"Twenty-two, I think," she grinned.

"And you know a twenty-two-year-old, how?"

Treena laughed, "Good grief, girl, why does it matter? He gets me booze."

***

Grabbing a handful of chips from the bowl on the counter by the basement stairs, Derrick tossed them into his mouth as he and Collin rehashed football wins from the prior season. He glanced towards the stairs when he heard the sounds of girls' giggles. Treena and Jessica entered the room, and Collin jabbed Derrick in the ribs with his elbow. Derrick gave him a wary look. Slapping him on the back, Collin said, "Whatever, pal," and headed over to the girls.

 "Welcome ladies," Collin said, moving in between the two girls and wrapping his arms around their waists while glancing over at Derrick and winking. Derrick turned his body back toward the snack counter. *Collin always knows how to greet the ladies,* he thought. *But he needs to keep his paws off Jessica.* Wiping the potato chip grease on his pant leg and feigning interest in the titles of the books that were on a shelf beside the counter.

"Treena, what cha got in the bag?" Derrick heard Collin ask.

Treena grinned and held open her oversized purse, and Collin peered inside.

"I have just the place for that," he smiled, releasing his grip from Jessica and steering Treena to the opposite side of the basement.

Having spotted Derrick as soon as she stepped into the basement, Jessica quietly walked up behind him. "Boo," she said, and briefly grabbed him by the waist and lightly squeezed. "Get a load of this place, huh Der?" She smiled up at him.

"Yeah, I think my entire house would fit in just this basement."

"Where are his parents? Do they know he's having this party?"

"Yeah, they know. At least his mom does. I saw her when I came in. He pretty much gets to do whatever he wants, especially when his dad is out of town, and he told me he went to Boston for the week."

"When Treena and I got here there was a note on the door saying head to the basement. Good thing Treena knew where the basement was. Geez, you could get lost in this place."

"Did I hear my name?" Treena asked, coming around the corner smiling, her hands sporting two red solo cups. "Here," Treena said, holding a cup towards Jessica.

Looking Treena in the eye, Jessica said dryly, "What's in it?"

"Punch, fruit punch, full of vitamin C. Drink up!"

"What else?"

Derrick brow furrowed as he squinted his eyes, watching the exchange between the two girls.

"Nothing! now relax, it's a party." Treena said holding her drink in the air, "Whoo! Whoo! Let's get some tunes going and get this party started!" She grabbed Jessica's arm and pulled her across the room where an iPod was sitting in a docking station, the music barely audible.

Laughing, Jessica allowed herself to be dragged along. She turned her head to Derrick and mouthed *later* in his direction.

Treena scrolled through the song list, cranked up the volume, and began head bobbing to a rap Jessica wasn't familiar with. Some of Treena's friends gathered around them, and soon others joined. Jessica looked around the room and saw it was filling up with a lot of faces she didn't know well. Most she had seen in the halls at school, but so far there wasn't anyone she felt like she could walk up and talk to. Looking over to the counter where she had left Derrick, she caught a glimpse of his back as he was walking out the sliding glass doors to a patio where she could see a group of kids. *What a house,* she once again thought.

She recalled entering the house at ground level but noted the basement opened to a vast backyard. She looked at the stairs, then at the patio doors and remembered her mom saying the house was built in a hill, and they had a pool, and a pool house for changing clothes and showering. Jessica considered going outside and hanging with Derrick, but she didn't know what she would say if he was talking with his football buddies. She walked over to a recliner and sat down and took a long drink of punch. *Surely this is straight punch,* she thought, looking at the cup. *Tastes like punch, and Treena knows I don't want to drink.* She took another long drink. Bored, she looked around the room at the nameless faces. *Why did I come here?*

Jessica put her empty cup on the table by her chair. She grabbed the throw pillow that was at her side and put it on her lap and absent-mindedly played with the fringe around the edges while watching Treena and her girlfriends dance. She recognized Sara from FCA. *Wow, I never would have pegged her as a party girl,* Jessica thought, watching the girls throwing their arms in the air and wiggling their butts. Jessica laughed out loud before quickly putting her hand over her mouth. *Why can't I just get up and join them?* Jessica looked at her empty cup. *Maybe if I have just one drink with booze, I could join them without feeling stupid. Maybe it would loosen me up a little.* She looked at the girls then looked around the room. *No one seems to care that they're acting silly, and they do look like they are having a good time.*

Treena danced over to Jessica and reached out her hand and grabbed her arm.

"Come on, get up and shake your bootie!"

Jessica, pulling her arm back replied, "Maybe later," and picked up the pillow that had fallen from her lap when Treena grabbed her.

"Suit yourself," Treena said, dancing her way back to the group of girls who were now joined by several of the guys she recognized from the football team.

"Oh, hell," Jessica said, grabbing her cup and getting up from the chair. *Whoa,* she thought, *I must have gotten up too quickly.* Feeling a little light headed she walked to the snack area. Grabbing a handful of chips, she stood by the table eating them and perusing the pitchers on the table. "Hmm, now which one should I have. They all look like Hawaiian Punch to me. Enny meeny minney moe," she said while pointing to each one. After filling her glass from the next to last pitcher, she took a long drink. Feeling a slight burn as the liquid hit her stomach, she thought, *Me thinks this is more than punch. Me thinks what Treena gave me earlier was more than punch.* Giggling, she thought, *Oh, what the heck, I was fine with those drinks at the football game. Actually, I think I had fun.* She looked around the room, then topped off her cup and walked over to the table by the music.

"Hey, there's my girl!" Treena smiled, grabbed Jessica's hand and pulled her towards the throng of gyrating teens. Dropping her grasp on Jessica, she danced her way to the middle of the group, smiling and pointing towards Jessica and back towards the dancers while continuing to gyrate her way amidst the crowd.

Staying on the fringes, Jessica took a long drink from her cup. Peering over the top at the mass of kids that now filled the room, she thought, *how in the heck does Collin know so many people?* Lowering her glass, she nodded towards Sara who had her hands in the air and was tossing her head back and forth as her feet gracefully moved in steps that made her look like she could be on "Dancing with the Stars". Sara grinned back. "Hey Jessica, come on, let's dance!" Setting her cup on a nearby table, she did her best to dance her way to Sara.

"That's it, come on girl!" Sara grabbed her hand and twirled her in a circle.

Jessica laughed. *This could be fun,* she thought, beginning to mimic the movements around her.

"Just go with the flow. Feel the music!" Sara closed her eyes and moved her body to the rhythm of the music.

Jessica looked at the crowd; some dancing, some standing in groups talking, and others at the other end of the basement where she could see the wall-sized television that sported a Wii game of bowling in progress. Suddenly, she realized no one cared what she was doing, and like Sara, she closed her eyes and let the music take over, moving her body to the beat.

***

"Hey, lookin' good, girlfriend!" Carolyn said, sizing up Missy who had just hopped in the car and was adjusting her seat belt.

"Yeah, check out these girls," Missy beamed and attempted to shimmy back and forth beneath the restraints of the seat belt. "Not so much bounce for the ounce anymore! That's a good thing, right?"

"Yeah," Carolyn inwardly smiled, "that's a good thing."

I guess that depends on one's objective, RB thought as she fluttered in the breeze, anxious to get to the party.

***

As the two friends walked down the stairs towards the basement, Carolyn turned towards Missy. "Behave yourself, okay?"

"What do you mean?" Missy replied, feeling a little chagrined like she was being reprimanded by an adult instead of getting ready to party with a friend.

"Oh, nothing, sorry." *I should keep my big fat mouth shut,* Carolyn thought as they entered the basement. *I just hope she doesn't get drunk and try to show off her new bra, or worse, what's under her bra.* Carolyn knew the other girls on the squad didn't like Missy, and she also knew they didn't want her at the party. She had practically begged the girls to give her a chance and try to see past her flamboyant ways. Carolyn recalled a conversation she had with Kim when she found out Missy was trying out for the squad. She said her boyfriend, Joe, told her Missy would 'do' anyone on the football team. Carolyn knew Missy tended to act pretty loose around the guys, but she didn't think she went all the way. At least Missy never confided in her if she did. *Like Kim and Joe aren't doin' it,* she thought, entering the basement and waving across the room to Kim, who had her arms wrapped around Joe, her tongue dancing around his ear.

Kim unwrapped herself from Joe's torso and hollered at Carolyn.

Carolyn waved back. "Hey," she said to Missy, "I'm gonna go talk to Kim, you okay?"

"Sure!" Missy knew she was being dismissed. She also knew most of the girls didn't like her, especially Kim. Putting a big smile on her face, she nodded towards the snack table. "Think I'll go find something to snack on. Want anything?"

"Nah, I'll get something later."

Missy stood surveying the mixture of chips and candies when she heard someone walk up behind her. While turning to see who it was, her elbow brushed their side.

"Hey, want some candy, little girl?"

Missy looked up at Joe, standing before her with a lascivious grin on his face.

"You really need to get a better line. That may work with Kim, but not me," Missy retorted, picking up a red M&M and popping it in her mouth while nodding in the direction of Kim and Carolyn. "You sure you want to leave your little girl unattended? Looked to me like she wanted some action from you a few minutes ago. Whatsa matter, can't Miss Cheerleader Captain satisfy you?" Missy gave him a tight-lipped grin.

Joe leaned in closer to Missy, his breath filling her air with the smell of beer. She stood her ground and didn't budge when he leaned in closer, his lips brushing against her ear as he whispered, "You just wait. I'll show you things the rest of the team never dreamed of doing." He shot his tongue out and licked her earlobe, then turned and walked towards the door leading to the patio.

Missy stood perfectly still for a few minutes, resisting the urge to wipe her ear. She watched Joe go outside where no doubt the beer cooler was hidden in the bushes, or maybe even out in the open because it didn't appear Collin's parents gave a hoot about under-age drinking. She glanced over to where Carolyn and Kim were standing, now surrounded by the other cheerleaders and some kids she recognized from her lit class. *Screw up one time,* she thought, *and you're branded for life.* She briefly thought back to the summer when she was still in junior high, and her mother had a tryst with 'The Pervert'. Missy shuddered at the thought as she looked around the table for some booze and once again berated herself for the way she behaved after that. *Ah,* she thought, spying the ubiquitous pitchers of fruit punch that seemed to fool the parents at every party. Grabbing a cup, she filled it to the brim, squelching her memories as she took a long, satisfying drink.

Uh, oh, RB thought, *I sure hope Carolyn doesn't leave her alone too long. And what a scumbag that Joe fella is! Ewww!*

"That Missy's a hot one!" Joe loudly proclaimed, walking toward the cooler in search of a Budweiser. He grabbed a beer and screwed off the top, tossing it to the ground where it landed at Derrick's feet. Derrick bent down and picked it up.

"Come on, man, show some respect."

"What, you got the hots for Missy?" Joe snickered before taking a long pull from his bottle.

"No, man, what are you talking about? Don't throw your trash on the ground, geez."

"What, are you the litter patrol or something?"

"Hey, like I said, just show a little respect. You really think we're going to keep getting to have parties here if the place is littered with beer caps?"

"Duh, with the money they have I'm sure the hired help doesn't care. Loosen up Der, have a drink," Joe said, holding his bottle towards Derrick.

Derrick, ignoring Joe's offer, turned and walked to the door, tossing the bottle cap in a nearby trash can on his way.

"What a puss!" Joe loudly proclaimed to the group of guys standing around the fire pit.

Walking in the house, Derrick glanced at the group of kids dancing. He did a double take when he saw Jessica whooping it up, a drink in her hand, the liquid sloshing out and hitting her arm. He watched her as she giggled and licked the red liquid from her arm while she continued to dance. He began to walk over to her but stopped when he saw Chuck lean in and lick a red drop of liquid that was dripping off her elbow. *What the heck,* he thought, confused by what he was seeing. *Jessica doesn't drink.* Then he saw Treena dancing towards them, noticeably drunk, her drink sloshing as she threw her arms around them both, and they began a three-way hip bopping back and forth.

Missy, still standing by the snacks, observed Derrick's reaction to Jessica, temporarily distracting her thoughts from Joe's unsolicited advances. She knew they had been friends forever, and she wondered if they had a thing going. Taking another long drink, she reached up and grasped a strand of hair, twirling it in her fingers while contemplating how to approach Derrick. Sighing, she reminded herself he wasn't interested in her. Her sigh turned into a grin as her thoughts turned to how she toyed with him in lit class. *Maybe, just maybe, someday he will be interested*, she thought before reaching up and self-consciously wiping her ear, revulsion growing in the pit of her stomach recalling Joe's comment. She fleetingly thought about how the rumor that involved her and the football team happened. *Junior high football team*, she silently corrected herself as shame began to creep into her soul, thinking about her role in the making of the rumor. She shook her head and consciously shoved the memories into the Pandora Box she kept in her brain to hold the unspeakable truths she rarely let slip out and into her conscious thoughts. She looked over at Derrick. *He wasn't like the rest of the guys, but he didn't start playing football until high school*, she thought, mentally tightening the latch on Pandora's Box, sufficiently snuffing out the memories. She had a feeling if she could get him alone, if he could see her for the person she actually was, maybe they could be something. She continued to twirl her hair as she watched his reaction to Jessica. Missy was a little surprised to see her dancing, and with Chuck of all people! Wow, surely he didn't just lick her elbow? *Hmm. I just may have a chance with Derrick.* Missy smiled at the thought.

Derrick turned from the dance floor, his stomach in knots. He walked towards the snacks but stopped when he saw Missy standing in front of the table, twirling her hair and staring at him. *Oh, boy,* he thought, *this I don't need right now.* Abruptly, he stopped, turned and faced the television, the Wii game frozen on the screen, and the players sitting on the couch drinking beer.

Missy took a quick drink and strolled up to Derrick as he walked away. "Hey Derrick," she called to him. As much as he wanted to ignore her and keep walking towards the guys, Derrick turned and looked at her. He wasn't raised to be rude, and he figured he could deflect anything Missy tossed his way.

"Some party, huh?" she said, nodding towards the dancers.

"Uh, yeah, hey, I need to go talk to Mason," Derrick said, turning to walk away.

"Wait," Missy said, reaching out and touching his arm. "You were really great out there on the field last night."

"Thanks," Derrick said, taking a step back in an attempt to remove Missy's hand from his arm.

Missy grasped his arm and looked up at him. "I'm a cheerleader now." *Geez,* she thought as soon as the words were out of her mouth, *how lame is that.*

"Yeah, I know. Good for you. Now I really need to go talk to Mason."

"Sure, well, I'll go with you," Missy said, releasing her grip on his arm and quickly hooking it around his.

Oh, man, how did she manage that? Derrick thought. *I'll never hear the end of it from the guys.* He tried to disengage her arm, but she only clung tighter while looking up at him and smiling. He returned her grin with a surly smile. Missy threw her head back and laughed. "Lighten up Der; it's party time!"

RB, watching the scenario take place, shook her straps as she watched Missy shamelessly throw herself at Derrick. *She is acting like such a skank! I hope Derrick can shake her loose before Jessica sees them, but then again, Jessica certainly isn't doing anything to encourage Derrick! What is wrong with these kids!*

***

Jessica, who was being twirled in circles by Chuck, the tips of her fingers barely touching his as he held their arms high and she swirled beneath them, caught a glimpse of Derrick and Missy heading towards the couch. Stopping in mid swirl, her mouth dropped open as she stared at them. Chuck, following her glance, grabbed her and pulled her close. Jessica began to resist, but then she saw Missy throw her head back and laugh. *I can't believe he's hooking up with that dirty slut,* she thought. Pulling Chuck close, she laid her head on his chest, allowing him to hold her tightly as they swayed back and forth to the music.

Oh, crap, RB thought, realizing Jessica did indeed see Derrick and Missy.

"Whoa, look at you," Mason shouted out as Derrick and Missy approached the couch.

Shooting him a dirty look, Derrick twisted his arm, deftly removing himself from Missy's clutches.

"Wha' up man?" Mason said to Derrick as he looked Missy up and down, his red-rimmed eyes doing little to hide the lust behind them.

Smiling sweetly, Missy's face belied her true thoughts. She flashed back to the hot summer night, the year before seventh grade. Mason didn't have the muscular build he now sported. He was just a fat, pimply kid. She shook her head attempting to erase the memory. Strands of blonde hair briefly floated effortlessly before falling across her eyes. Lifting her hand to sweep the hair to the side, her smile turned into a glare, warning Mason to back off. It was an unspoken secret they had all kept, yet she wondered if the guys talked about it when they were alone - or drunk.

"Nothin' other than I'm gonna whoop your butt bowling," Derrick said, stepping further away from Missy and picking up the Wii controller.

"Ah, bowling is for sissies, how 'bout some Halo?" Mason said as he made several attempts to lift himself from the couch. "Why don't you be a babe and go get us some brews," Mason said, turning his attention towards Missy.

"I'm not your babe, asshole."

Mason grinned from ear to ear. "I sthink I'm in love," he slurred, making another attempt to lift himself from the sagging cushions of the couch. Bouncing off the couch, he stumbled in her direction. Missy took a step backward, barely missing being tackled by the obnoxious mass heading her way.

"Hey," Derrick said pointing the game controller towards Mason, "your turn."

Mason looked from Missy towards Derrick, then back to Missy. "Ah, who wants used goods anyway," he sneered, grabbing the controller from Derrick's hand and stumbling towards the television. "Game on!"

Her eyes brimming with tears, Missy turned, willing herself not to cry. Walking back to the snack table she kept her eyes cast down, her vision blurry from the tears welling in them and resting on her lower lashes. Raising her head, she looked down at the food and drink, and a tear rolled down her cheek. Seeing Sara approaching, she quickly wiped it off with the heel of her hand. Sara looked at her quizzically for a moment then reached out her hand.

THE RED BRA

"Hey, I'm Sara, you're Missy, right?" Missy stared at her hand, unsure what was expected. *Since when do girls shake hands when they meet?* she wondered as she tentatively reached out her hand. Sara's grasp was firm, and she smiled a genuine smile as she looked Missy in the eye.

"Yeah, I think I've seen you around," Missy said, wary of an upperclassman trying to make nice with her.

"Some party, huh?"

Missy stared blankly at her, not sure if she was about to be the butt of someone's joke, or if this girl was genuine.

"Didn't expect so much booze, though," Sara continued. "Geez, can't believe Collin's mom doesn't even check up on anyone. "Wow, Look at those girls on the dance floor! It is entertaining, but I have a feeling I'll be making several trips tonight driving them home."

"Oh, you drew the short straw?"

"Excuse me?"

"You know, you were picked to be the DD."

RB perked up when she heard, DD, and began paying attention to the conversation between Sara and Missy.

"Oh, no, I never drink. Never had the desire. Besides, it's against the law," Sara said as she nonchalantly picked up a handful of M&M's and began tossing them into her mouth.

Now I remember who she is, Missy thought. *She's that goody-two-shoes president of the FCA. Probably wandered over here to save my soul. Well, too late.*

"Didn't I see you whooping it up on the dance floor earlier?" Missy inquired.

"Sure did! Hey, you don't have to drink to let loose and have some fun. Besides," she leaned in towards Missy as if she were going to impart a deep dark secret, "from what I hear, hangover anxiety is no fun." Sara straightened and grabbed another handful of M&M's. "Good snacks, huh?"

"Uh, yeah, but I was looking for something to drink."

"There's soda in the fridge," Sara said, pointing to the silver Amana against the far wall. "I could use some caffeine myself," she said, gently grasping Missy's arm and steering her towards the refrigerator. "Grab some cups."

Missy handed the cups to Sara and silently watched her fill them with ice and soda.

"I noticed you're on the cheering squad. Good for you! How do you like it?" Sara asked, handing Missy her cup.

"It's great! Better than I ever imagined." She almost added that it would be even better now that her boobs would stay put, but she didn't think Sara was the type to want to have that kind of conversation.

"You should join FCA."

Missy creased her brow and cocked her head while giving Sara a blank stare.

"You know, Fellowship of Christian Athletes."

Considering how to respond, Missy took a long drink of her soda. She was glad Sara got her a soda. She tried not to drink too much as she didn't always like the person she became when she drank, even if it did temporarily dull the empty places inside of her. *Funny that Sara should mention hangover anxiety,* she thought, grimacing and recalling the nights she couldn't completely remember. *Guess I'm not the only one who has had that affliction.*

"Um, well, I don't belong to a church."

"That doesn't matter. It's just a bunch of kids getting together to praise our individual higher power. It's pretty uplifting. Seriously, stop in for a meeting. There's no pressure to join or share or anything like that. We read the bible and pray, but we also talk about the sports we're in, and we help each other out with problems. We meet in Mr. Johnson's room at seven before school every Wednesday. Oh, and you get free doughnuts." She smiled. "Guess I better go check on my besties. Nice chatting." Sara gave a short wave before heading back to the dance floor.

Wow, that was interesting, Missy thought, looking around the room for Carolyn. *I'm so ready to leave this party. Where the heck is she?* Spotting some girls from the cheerleading squad, she walked over to them.

"You know where Carolyn is?"

The girls, pointedly ignoring her, continued their conversation. Missy folded her arms across her chest and stared at them. "I asked you a question."

Brandy turned her head towards Missy, "Moi? You espeaking to moi? No comprende." The girls broke into a cacophony of laughter.

"Grow up," Missy scoffed then turned on her heel and headed to the sliding glass doors and the patio beyond.

Well, little Miss Greer, RB wryly thought, *me thinks the hoity-toity cheerleaders don't like you much! I think I better follow along and keep an eye on you.*

Stepping outside, Missy let out a deep sigh as the cool evening air hit her face. *Why did I ever think being on the squad would make them like me?* She pulled back her foot to kick at one of the bottle caps that were strewn on the ground, but instead of following through, she bent over and began to pick them up. She walked to the trash can by the door just as Derrick was stepping outside. She looked up at him while dropping the caps in the trash.

"There are some litter-bugs around here," she said with a sheepish grin before turning and walking over to the concrete benches that were placed strategically around the patio. She knew Derrick's opinion of her wasn't any different than that of the girls on the squad. As she sat down on the cold hard bench, she could hear Derrick laughing and telling the guys by the beer cooler something or another about Mason being falling down drunk. *Duh,* Missy thought, leaning back and looking at the sky. H*opefully, he's passed out. What a moron.*

Trying to empty her mind, she looked towards the full moon which cast a sensuous glow on the landscape below. She began to relax and enjoy her surroundings. She could hear the chirping of frogs in the distance, giving one last chorus before winter hit and they burrowed themselves deep in the mud. She remembered one of her science teachers telling the class frogs had antifreeze in their blood or something. *Why do I remember that?* she mused while admiring the immaculately kept yard.

She closed her eyes and daydreamed about what it would be like to marry someone who could provide her with a home and yard of this magnitude. She could see the pool off to the side, and after a time she got up and walked down the cobblestone path and through a vine-covered pergola. She couldn't help but marvel at the magnificence of the place. The path ended at an ornate black wrought iron fence that surrounded the pool. She debated opening it and going in to check it out even though she could see the pool was covered for the upcoming winter months. She stood leaning on the fence, lost in her thoughts of a knight in shining armor whisking her away to a place such as this when she heard a commotion behind her. Stepping to the side and turning around she saw Jessica's arms flailing through the air and slapping at Derrick. He had one arm in the air shielding himself and was backing up as she continued to stumble towards him waving her arms and shouting incoherently.

Oh, wow, looky here, Jessica is bombed! Missy leaned back against the fence to watch the show. She strained to make out what was being said.

"How could you be with her? Huh? How could you?"

Derrick reached out and grabbed her arms and held them to her side. "What are you talking about Jess?

"Don't act like you don't know. I saw you with her arm around you!" Jessica said, struggling to free herself from Derrick's grasp.

Oh, crap, did I hear right? Missy thought. *I guess they do have a thing for each other. Crap, here I go, always messing things up for everyone.* Silently, Missy moved into the shadows for fear of being seen. From her new vantage point, she couldn't see what was going on, but she thought she heard Derrick say it wasn't his doing. Missy held her breath, afraid someone would see her. She could hear Jessica crying and Derrick making some kind of nicey nice noises to her. Hearing the sliding doors open, she peered out from the shadows to see Derrick guiding a staggering, simpering Jessica back into the house. *And that,* she said to herself, *is why I limit my alcohol. Well, at least attempt to. Sure am glad I ran into that Sara chick or who knows what I would have done. Maybe I will go to one of those goody-two-shoes meetings. Free doughnuts, right?* She inwardly grinned before chortling out loud.

Oh, wow! I didn't see that coming, RB thought hovering about the patio. *I knew Treena was bad news!*

Missy walked back to the concrete bench and sat down slowly, wondering how long she should wait before going inside and continuing her search for Carolyn. She sure as heck didn't want to run into Derrick or Jessica. Nice guy that he was, he was probably driving her home or fixing her a pot of coffee. A group of guys was still standing around the beer cooler, and she couldn't make out what they were saying, but by the sounds of their guffaws and laughter, she figured they were probably telling lies or dirty jokes. *No doubt I'm the butt of their jokes,* she thought before tuning them out and leaning back on the bench to continue her daydreams of a better life and a wealthy future. She was so caught up in her fantasy she didn't hear Carolyn approach.

"There you are!" Carolyn said, "I've been looking all over for you. What are you doing out here by yourself?"

"Actually, I came out here looking for you. Where you been?"

"Oh, do you know Laurie? Short, brown hair, freckles?"

"Um, no, don't think so."

"Well, she goes to my church, and we know each other mostly from youth group. She's younger than us. I was kinda surprised to see her here, but she's friends with Joanie. She's having boy problems, and we went upstairs to sit and talk."

"Okay, fun times for you, huh?"

"Ah, that's okay, this party's kinda lame anyway. I don't know what I expected, but I sure didn't expect to see so many kids getting wasted. Geez, what do their parents think when they get home? I'd be grounded for life if I came home drunk or smelling like booze." Carolyn paused and arched an eyebrow while looking intently at Missy. "You been drinking?"

177

"Nah, well, maybe one when we first got here, but your friend, Sara, cornered me and made me drink a soda. She invited me to an FCA meeting, and I may go."

"Yeah! The donuts are delish!"

That Carolyn sure has a steady head for a teenager! RB thought. *Doesn't drink, counsels friends, goes to church, but most importantly, she buys bras for those in need! Talk about a supportive friend! I better go check up on Jessica. Now she's one that could use Carolyn's sensibilities about now.*

Derrick pulled up in front of Jessica's house, but not before he had pulled over not once, but twice, so she could puke. *Good thing we live in the country,* Derrick thought, digging his hand in the McDonald's bag for a napkin so she could wipe her face before she went in the house. He was angry with her, but he also felt guilty. *If I hadn't let Missy wrap her arm around me, this never would have happened.* He banged his fist on the steering wheel. Startled, Jessica looked over at him. Between the coffee and the sandwich from McDonald's, she was starting to sober up even though her food and drink were now fodder for the raccoons and possums.

"I'm sorry, Der. I don't know what got into me."

"Yeah, well, tell that to your folks. You know they're going to know you've been drinking."

Jessica looked towards the house. She could see the kitchen light on, but the rest of the house was dark.

178

"They should be in bed. Have you seen my purse?"

"Yeah, Treena found it. Here," he said, shoving the crumpled McDonald's bag to the side and slightly lifting it."

"Thanks," Jessica mumbled before opening it up and scrounging through it for a piece of gum. Slowly she unwrapped the gum and popped it in her mouth. "I'm really sorry."

Derrick sat silently with both hands on the wheel staring straight ahead. With her eyes cast downward, Jessica got out of the truck and made her way towards the door.

Derrick drove away slowly, keeping his eye in the mirror until he saw her open the door. Once she was out of sight, he gunned the engine causing the truck to fishtail before speeding down the dirt road towards home.

Oh, boy, RB thought, arriving just in time to see Jessica's down-trodden walk to the door and the dust trail behind Derrick's truck. *These kids may be over before they have a chance to begin. Booze in control - not a good thing.*

***

Missy got out of Carolyn's car and walked across the yard to her own house. A few steps into the yard she noticed the Harley sitting in her driveway. *Oh, great, Mom bagged another man,* she thought, slowing her pace to the house. She glanced back towards Carolyn's house and considered asking to spend the night there, but Carolyn had already gone in, and their living room light had turned off. Missy stood at the door with her key in her hand, straining her ears for any sound. *How bad is it that I hope they are in bed, so I don't have to deal?* she silently thought. *Oh, just get it over with. Not like it's anything new.* Missy entered the living room to a plethora of empty beer cans scattered on the coffee table and stacked in a pyramid on the end table. *Cute,* she grimaced. *They would have fit right in at Collin's party.* Silently, she walked to her room, thankful her mother's door was closed. Missy began undressing for bed and stood silently in front of the mirror for a minute admiring her new bra. Smiling, she turned sideways and grinned, pleased at how her breasts looked with their new accommodations. *Who would have thunk a new bra could make such a difference?* she mused, removing her bra and noting for the first time in a very long time there were no harsh red marks on her skin showing the bra's imprint. Slipping on an oversized t-shirt, she said a silent thank you to Carolyn before crawling between the crisp sheets on her bed. Just as she was drifting off to sleep, she was startled by a loud noise coming from the direction of her mother's bedroom. Bolting upright in bed, her heart pounded, her hands instantly became clammy, and her mouth grew dry. *Please God,* she silently prayed, *don't let this one be a beater... or a pervert,* she added to her prayers after a pause. She tried to squelch the memories that came flooding into her consciousness as she lay down and

180

covered her head with her pillow attempting to block the sounds of fighting and memories of 'The Pervert'. She could feel her face redden as she lay in the dark; shame and disgust fighting for equal time in her brain. *I was just a kid,* she thought, fighting to keep the tears from flowing. *I should have told someone who would listen.* She did her best to turn off the instant replay that kept repeating itself in her mind of the day she tried to tell her mother. She lay still, trying not to listen to the drunken accusations being tossed about in the other room, her thoughts ricocheting from the night of 'The Pervert' to her own actions soon after. She inhaled a deep breath of air as she became aware that she had been holding her breath since hearing the crash of what sounded like the beer can pyramid tumbling. She steadied her breathing and heard the door slam, then the sounds of her mother kicking empty beer cans. *And another one bites the dust,* she thought, trying hard to add some levity to another one of her mother's mishaps.

RB's straps sagged, and her cups drooped. *Well, that explains a lot,* she thought while silently lifting herself high towards the moonlit sky and sailing into the night.

***

Derrick bowed his head in prayer with the rest of his family that was gathered at the table for their ritual Sunday after church brunch. While his father said the traditional blessing, he added his own prayer of thanks that Jessica wasn't in church that morning. He didn't know what to say to her, and he was confused about his feelings. He had calmed down from his initial anger at her for being drunk and for dancing and acting stupid with Chuck. He even understood her drunken hand slapping and tongue lashing. He couldn't help but give a wry smile, recalling her attack. He hadn't seen her that mad since they were eight years old, and he snitched her brownie at lunch. How was he supposed to know she had been thinking about that brownie all morning while the teacher droned on about how to add twelve plus two? *I should tell her that,* he thought, his grin widening, but just as quickly he became somber, and his mouth tightened. He had envisioned an evening of them talking and maybe dancing. He had hoped to hold her close during a dance and somehow let her know his feelings for her. But she showed up with Treena who pulled her away and gave her booze. Then Missy did her thing. *Oh, boy,* he thought, scooping some scrambled eggs on his plate, *I lost before I began.*

"What's up little bro'?" Darnell asked, observing the conflicting emotions flickering across Derrick's face.

Derrick scowled at him, "Don't call me that."

"Okay, no offense meant, you just don't seem yourself."

"Sorry, everything's fine," Derrick said, lifting a forkful of eggs and potatoes to his mouth while giving Darnell a sour look.

Darnell, not one to back down, continued talking in an effort to draw him out. "Okay, any chance you've changed your mind about riding with me to look at that tractor? Or do you still have other plans?" he asked with a smile and a wink.

Derrick stared blankly at Darnell, *Oh, crud,* he thought. *I forgot all about our plans to study for the test together today. That is if Jessica still wants to.* Derrick briefly considered going with Darnell so he would have a good excuse for not meeting up with her. He wondered if she wasn't at church because she was too hung over, or because she didn't want to see him. *Probably both,* he thought.

"Um, yeah, I still have plans," Derrick said, forcing a smile but not knowing if he did or not.

Well, maybe there is still hope for these two, RB thought as she arrived, refreshed from a night of meandering the countryside.

Derrick finished his meal in silence, excused himself, went to his room, and stretched out on his bed. Staring at the ceiling, he thought about his options. *Do nothing. Text her. Just show up. Just show up wouldn't be good. Maybe she wasn't at church because she really was sick. Yeah, right. Do nothing. Maybe, but that will just prolong things. I guess I should text her and act like nothing's wrong.* He sat up and grabbed his phone.

what time u want 2 study

183

He stared at the words for a full minute, wondering if he should ask her if she still wanted to study. *No, I need to man up and just lay it out there, go over there and let her know I want to be more than just friends. I can do this.* He hit send.

***

Jessica stepped out of the shower and heard the whoosh of her phone. Picking it up from the vanity, she stared at the words Derrick had written. A smile slowly crept across her face. *He still wants to see me!* Reading the words again, she felt butterflies in her stomach. She was intensely ashamed of her actions and prayed she didn't get any puke in his truck. She had only been up a few hours and had spent most of the time berating herself for drinking, for dancing with Chuck, for slapping Derrick, for puking, and for whatever else she did that she couldn't remember. Her cheeks grew red as she once again recalled the scene she made outside at Collin's. *Well, I guess he knows I like him, but he sure was pissed when he dropped me off. I've never seen him that mad.* Jessica quickly dressed and went to her room. She looked at the clock and noted it was a little after two. She was surprised at how much better she felt. She sure felt awful when her mother tried to get her up for church. She told her mom she was awake most of the night because she had too much caffeine at the party, and she let her stay home and sleep. Recalling the lie, she briefly wondered if it was a double sin if your lie was to get out of going to church.

Her heart pounding, she picked up her phone.

3 ok?

She hit send before she could change her mind.

Derrick, still holding the phone in his hand, smiled when he saw her reply

c u soon

He responded, a wide grin stretching across his face.

Oh yes! These two are meant to be together! RB thought, playfully clapping her straps together.

***

Derrick wiped his sweaty palms on his pant leg before knocking on Jessica's door. He took a deep breath and quelled his nerves by thinking about how she was probably feeling. He was glad she agreed to meet. He hoisted his backpack up to his shoulder, and as he lifted his hand to knock again the door opened, and Jessica stood before him. She smiled and held the door wide for him to enter.

"Hey, you ready to fill your brain with ancient history?"

"If that's what I have to do to keep you from wasting paper. You know, trees are a valuable resource," she smiled back, recounting Mr. Johnson's admonishment in history class.

They walked into the dining room where Jessica had already put her books and notes. Derrick lifted his backpack and put it on the table. Jessica turned to Derrick and looked straight at him. Unexpected tears began to well in her eyes. "Der," she paused and took a deep breath as one lone tear found its way between her lashes and rolled down her cheek.

"Shh," Derrick said, gently putting his hands on her arms. He rubbed his hands up and down her arms as she looked towards the ceiling to stop more tears from falling. Derrick slid his arms around her back and pulled her close to him. She wrapped her arms around him, and they stood embraced, neither saying a word. Derrick inhaled the scent of her freshly washed hair and felt her heart beating against his. It was the best minute of his life. Jessica let out a deep breath and sighed, loosened her grasp, and stepped slightly away from him.

"You forgive me?" she asked.

Derrick, not saying a word, reached over to the table and unzipped his backpack. He reached in and picked up a small cellophane package and handed it to her.

"Do you forgive me?" he responded, handing her a brownie.

THE RED BRA

***

Missy rolled over and reached for the button on her alarm clock. 6:00 glared at her with its red numbers blinking and chastising her with their brilliant flickering light. Throwing her pillow over her head, she asked herself for the umpteenth time why she told Sara she would go to the FCA meeting that morning. Carolyn was even surprised when she said she was going and warned her not to be late if she wanted to ride with her. Sitting up, Missy wiped the sleep from her eyes. She thought about the past few days and how on Monday morning everyone was whispering about Jessica's tantrum. She recalled how quickly they shut-up when Jessica and Derrick were spotted walking down the hall holding hands and grinning like love-sick puppies. *Well, I guess they can thank me for that one. Don't think I'd do too well with the farm life anyway.* She had been avoiding Derrick and scooted her desk forward to get farther away from him in Lit class. *I certainly don't want to turn out like my mother. Lord knows how many fights she caused with her unabashed flirting with men who were already in relationships. That is not going to be me,* she thought, heading for the shower.

***

Missy and Carolyn walked into Mr. Johnson's classroom a few minutes before seven. Sara was opening a box of doughnuts, and her smile widened when she saw Missy.

"See, just like I said, doughnuts! Help yourself, and have some juice too," she said pointing to a jug of orange juice sitting next to the doughnuts.

"Mmm, yum," Carolyn said, walking over, grabbing a doughnut, and taking a big bite, oblivious to the tiny glazed sugar sheets falling on her blouse. "They're as good as they look. Fresh from the bakery!"

Missy smiled at her friend, and she picked up a doughnut. Looking around the classroom she saw the desks had been moved to form a circle, and students were starting to come in and take a seat.

"Come on, let's grab a seat," Carolyn said, walking towards the desks.

Missy sat down and looked around to see if anyone she knew was there, particularly any of the other cheerleaders. Her glance stopped when she saw Brandy blabbing away to a tall guy. *Probably a basketball player,* she surmised. *Hmm, she's a Christian? Could have fooled me the way she talked to me at the party.* Missy averted her glance when Brandy turned her way. *I'm better than that. I can be much better than that. No longer am I going to throw mean words back. From now on I will kill them with kindness.* Missy looked up and smiled sweetly at Brandy who was staring directly at her. Missy took a bite of doughnut then gently brushed the sugar from her turtleneck. *No more showing off the girls,* she thought, pleased she found a turtleneck shirt in the back of her closet. True, it was a little snug, and with the new bra, it did accentuate her breasts nicely. Her smiled widened. Baby steps.

Wow! RB thought, *I hope Missy really has turned over a new leaf. If she follows the adage, 'act the way you want to be, and soon you will be the way you act', she'll be just fine. And I must say, the outline of my sister bra is stunning beneath that turtleneck!* With that, RB took off in search of a new adventure.

Time ceased to have meaning as she drifted to and fro admiring the plains in Kansas and the majestic Rocky Mountains in Colorado. She reminisced about her young buds, Riley, Sydney, and Julia. She felt secure in their abilities to grow and live fruitful lives. She sent hope from her soul to the universe that Missy would continue with her uplifting journey through life and that Jessica and Derrick's love would last forever. She sailed towards the west coast fantasizing about a permanent union for them when she spotted a wedding taking place. Slowly, she left her place amidst the clouds and arrived just as the bride and groom kissed.

Chapter 12
Jill and Todd

Todd and Jill smiled radiantly, their hands intertwined while walking down the rose petal covered aisle. Jill could barely contain her happiness as she gazed lovingly at her husband. She couldn't have asked for a more beautiful day. The sun's rays blessed them with its warmth as robins and cardinals chirped their approval in the background. They arrived at the edge of the veranda to greet the guests who had just witnessed their union. Looking up at Todd, she thought about the first time she saw him. She was a fifth-year senior at UCLA and had given up on the thought of meeting 'Mr. Right' at college. She had dated a few guys during her college years, but no one she felt was the 'forever' guy. Dedicated to her studies, she had spent most of her time writing papers and doing research. Her work-study job was in the library, and that suited her just fine since it gave her the opportunity to work on her studies when things were slow. She also liked helping other students find the books they needed. She couldn't remember a time when she didn't love books. Some of her favorite childhood memories were of sitting on the porch swing reading *The Box Car Children*.

It was during her last semester that Todd walked up to her in the library. Jill remembered glancing up from the paperwork she was organizing and staring into the most beautiful blue eyes she had ever seen. He held her gaze for several seconds before posing his request. Jill had never believed in love at first sight, but at that moment she felt there really could be such a thing. If she didn't know better, she would have sworn that all the electrons in her body were reaching out to him as she felt the hairs on her arms come to attention, seemingly straining to touch him.

"Are you okay, uh, Jill?"

Oh my god, he knows my name. How does he know my name? Her face took on a quizzical, yet slightly worried look.

As if reading her mind, Todd said, "Your name tag," pointing to the required tag stating her name above the words Library Clerk.

"Oh, yeah, sorry," Jill said, lifting her hand and briefly touching the tag while feeling a warm flush creep over her face.

"You sure you're ok? You look kind of, well, ill."

Oh, great, terrific first impression, dork, Todd thought, running his hand through his dark hair while trying to think of something suave to say.

"No, I'm fine. Sorry, it's been a long day. Truthfully, it's been a long semester, but hey, it's almost over, and then onward and upward to bigger and better things." Jill put on her best smile, "Now, what were you looking for?"

"Um," Todd silently cursed himself. *What is it I came in here for? My god, she is the most amazing looking woman*

I have ever seen. How could I have not ever seen her before? What the hell is wrong with me? He wiped his brow and felt the beads of sweat forming. "Uh, Dr. Goodson said he put a book back for me, Todd, Todd Matthews." He said while reaching his hand out for a handshake.

Jill stared mutely at his hand. Todd quickly pulled his hand back. "Uh, sorry, old habit. My parents' fault." He grinned. *Lame, lame lame. Again, what the hell is wrong with me?*

"Well, your parents sound like good people," Jill said, extending her hand, "Jill Walters."

Todd quickly wiped his hand on his pant leg before reaching out and grasping her hand in his. "Nice to meet you, Jill Walters."

Jill shook herself from her reverie as the receiving line thinned. She felt a sense of happiness unlike anything she had ever experienced.

Todd looked at his bride and gently squeezed her hand as the last guest congratulated them. Her smile was radiant, and it still amazed him that she loved him as much as he loved her. His thoughts drifted back to the first time they met. He grinned, remembering shaking her hand in the library, and his smile grew wider, recalling the sparks that flew between them during their first contact. His reverie was interrupted when Jill's sister, Mandy, approached them; her pregnant belly straining against the silky Maid of Honor gown. She smiled at Todd while putting her arm through Jill's.

"Time to tie up the bustle. I won't keep her long," Mandy said, steering Jill towards the house.

Oh, goody! It's about time I began a new adventure with a positive note! I do enjoy a good love story!" RB exclaimed, fluttering above.

After giving her a gentle kiss, Todd watched them walk to the house. His thoughts drifted back to the first day at the library. The day she said she was Jill Walters. Now, Jill Matthews.

***

Todd left the library and drove to his apartment with thoughts of Jill dominating his mind. He could have sworn sparks flew when their hands touched. *My god, I'm a few weeks away from getting my engineering degree. I have finals. I don't have room in my brain for romance. Besides, there's no such thing as love at first sight. But what the hell was that?* He grinned. *What could it hurt to go out for dinner? I should have asked her for her phone number. At least I know where she works.* Todd pulled into his driveway and found himself whistling as he walked in the door. His roommate, Jerry, was sitting on the couch, his textbooks scattered over the coffee table in front of him. He looked up when Todd walked in.

"What are you so happy about?"

"Ah, nothin'. Just having a good day."

"Okay, spill," Jerry said, taking his glasses off and leaning back on the couch.

Todd sat down in the chair opposite Jerry. He tried not to smile, but sitting back, he felt all the stress of the semester dissipate as his grin stretched across his face.

"It's a girl, isn't it?"

"What makes you say that? Can't I just be happy?"

"Don't give me that crap. What's her name?"

"Jill. Jill Walters."

"Oh my god. You are smitten!"

Todd looked at Jerry and laughed. "Smitten, what the hell kind of word is smitten?"

"You know, smitten, rhymes with kitten. Kitten, another name for pussy."

Todd picked up one of Jerry's notebooks and threw it at him. "There's something seriously wrong with you."

"Nay, I just spent too much time with Grandma Em. Smitten was one of her words. She's a hoot." He grinned, "One of her words too. Do you know that back in the 60's she burned her bra? She loves telling that story. Did you know they called it the degrading mindless-boob-girlie symbol?"

"And you're wasting brain cells remembering this, why?"

"Hey, conversation starter! Remember Ellie? The one that never wore a bra? When I first saw her at *The Hole*, guzzling a PBR straight from the can with her perky little titties showing through her top, I walked up to her and said, I see you were in Atlantic City in the sixties. She was like, Oh my god, yeah, right. She was totally impressed with my knowledge of bra burning in response to the Miss America Contest."

"Okay, Mr. Jeopardy, enough already. You do realize you are a total dork."

"Well, it got me laid." Jerry grinned and threw the notebook back at Todd.

Todd picked up the notebook and looked at Jerry. "How you always manage to pick up girls I'll never figure out. Man, if I tried something like that I'd probably get smacked."

"It's all in the delivery, my friend, all in the delivery."

"Yeah, right, you ever picked up a sober girl?"

"Hey, no fair, Ella's sober."

"Grandma Em, Ellie, Ella, What's up with you and the E girls. You got an Oedipus complex or something?"

"Hey, don't be dissin' on my Grandma, and besides, Oedipus was after his mother, not his grandma. So, did you ask this Jane girl out?"

"It's Jill, not Jane, and no. She works on campus at the library."

"I'm guessing you are going to start hanging out at the library now. Turn all bookwormish on me, hide out behind the encyclopedias and spy on Jill."

"No, for god sake, man, this isn't high school. I'm going to hide behind the law books." Todd laughed.

"You gotta be cool man. Walk in there and grab some brainiac books, lay them on the counter, and be like, good thing I brought my library card cuz I'm checking you out!"

"I'm thinking if you google the word dork, you're gonna see your picture. Are you serious man? How old are you anyway?"

"Um, 12? or is it 21? Why do you ask me such hard questions? You know my dyslexia screws with numbers." Jerry laughed. "Come on man, just go in there and ask her out. How hard can it be? What do you have to lose? Go for it. Oh, and for your information, you would see my face if you googled debonair, not dork," Jerry said, pushing his long black hair behind his ears.

"Oh yeah, you're debonair all right. You do know long hair went out in the seventies."

"Hey, the girls love it. You should try it. I don't see that crew cut of yours getting you any time with the ladies."

Todd ran his hand through his hair. "It's not a crew cut, so shut up. Let's see who gets a job first."

"Seems to me I got the girl first," Jerry smirked.

"Yeah, you got me on that front. But tell me, other than growing my hair long and telling stupid jokes, how do I get Jill to notice me?"

"Hmm, I'm guessing she's not in any of your classes."

"I think I would have noticed that," Todd said dryly.

"Hey, I think Ella said something about her friend, Brenda, doing a work-study at the library." Jerry grabbed his phone and began texting.

"Whoa, what are you doing?"

"Texting Ella. Come on, you want a date or not?"

Todd leaned back in his chair and stared at the ceiling. "I guess. But be nice."

"No prob, Buddy," Jerry said, tapping send on the phone.

"Wait a minute, what did you say?"

Jerry grinned. "I told her to tell her friend Brenda to tell Jill you had a big schlong."

"You ass hole," Todd said, jumping out of his chair and tackling Jerry while grasping for his phone.

"Hey, easy guy," Jerry laughed, holding his phone tightly in his hand. "The truth shouldn't hurt so much. I know you'll go easy on her."

"Give me the damn phone."

"Chill man, I just asked her if Brenda worked at the library. Geez, get a grip."

Todd released his hold on Jerry and stood up. "Sorry man, I just don't want to blow this."

"You want Jill to blow this," Jerry said, reaching out and trying to grab Todd's crotch.

Todd jumped back, "God, cool it. This is a nice girl. I'm not looking for a one-night stand here."

Todd fell back in the chair and propped his feet on the table at the same time Jerry's phone made the sound of a bomb exploding.

Todd jerked in his chair. "What the hell?"

Jerry snickered before looking at the text. "Cool, huh? Wait till you hear my new ringtone. I downloaded a bunch of new ones today. Do you know how many different sounds you can add to your phone? They're--"

Todd cut him off, "Just read the damn text."

"Uh yeah, right, my boy's in heat."

"Just read it."

Yes, y?

"Because I asked you to."

"No, you moron, that was Ella's response to my text. As in yes, Brenda works at the library, and why do I want to know."

"Oh, what do we say?"

"I'm guessing it's still a no to tell her to tell Jill about your, uh, appendage?"

"Come on; I really want to get to know this girl. Can you just be serious for a minute?"

"Ok, first things first." Jerry began to text.

"What are you doing?"

"Chill, just letting her know I'm asking for you, so she doesn't get all psycho on me. She's the jealous type." Jerry grinned at Todd and hit the send button. "What's she look like?"

"Oh man, she's beautiful! Short brownish blonde hair, blue eyes, about five six or so--"

Jerry cut him off. "Aw man, big tits, little tits, cute butt, flat butt?"

"Is that all you ever think about?"

"Well, now that you mention it, how about her legs? Do they go all the way up to her ass?"

"Matter of fact they do, just like everyone else, and her tits are perfect. Not too big, but definitely not too small."

"What are you talking here, a B cup?"

"How the hell do I know? I don't go around inspecting bras for size. They looked nice, and that's all I'm saying about that."

Jerry's fingers began dancing on his keypad.

"What are you doin'?"

"I'm asking Ella to ask Brenda to ask Jill what size bra she wears."

"You are twisted! Just leave it alone, will you!"

"I'm kidding. I asked her if she wanted to come over. I think you could use a girl's perspective on this, seeing as you're gettin' all girly on me."

A waiter carrying a tray of wine walked up to Todd shaking him from his reverie. Jerry approached from the opposite direction and slapped him on the back. "So happy for you, man!" he said as they each took a glass of wine. Jerry held his glass toward Todd's. "To eternal bliss. You both deserve it!"

***

While Mandy hooked Jill's bustle to the back of her wedding gown, she felt her baby kick. She stood and gazed lovingly at her little sister while gently rubbing her enormous belly.

"You look amazing," Mandy smiled at Jill. "I am incredibly happy for you. Now, let's get back out there. I'm sure your husband is anxious to be with his wife."

Seeing Jill, Todd nodded to Jerry and walked the few steps to meet her. They mingled with their guests during the cocktail hour and basked in all the love that surrounded them. Jill was thrilled to see how well the two families and all their friends cliqued. Smiling, she looked at Jerry and Ella chatting with her younger sister, Kendall, and her boyfriend, Sean. She and Ella had become fast friends after Brenda introduced them. Brenda had invited her out for drinks after work one evening. She almost didn't go, but Brenda assured her it was just a bunch of friends getting together for a celebratory drink after the last final. Jill had finished student teaching and decided she was in the mood to celebrate the end of her college career. She was ready to embrace life as a teacher, and she already had an interview scheduled for a fourth-grade position at the school where she student taught. She couldn't believe it when she saw Todd sitting at the table when she arrived. It wasn't until weeks later that Todd told her it was all a set-up so he could meet her. It was hard to believe that was three years ago.

Chapter 13
Wedding Reception

The dinner bell chimed, and the guests made their way to their assigned tables in the courtyard. The California weather was at its finest. A faint scent of the ocean wafted over the yard, bringing with it fond memories of sand castles and laughter from her youth, and more recently, moonlit walks with Todd. As a teenager growing up near the ocean, Jill had a recurring daydream of walking down the beach hand in hand with a handsome man. That dream had come true.

Music played softly in the background while the guests enjoyed their meal and the company of friends and family. Periodically someone would tap their glass, and the guests would pause to watch the bride and groom share a tender kiss, their faces glowing with love and promises of a bright future.

The guests finished their meals, and the tables were cleared. A band replaced the recorded music, and tables were moved to allow room for dancing. A warm, gentle breeze blew through the canopy as the bride and groom danced their first dance as husband and wife. The wine flowed while people mingled and danced. Old friends visited, and distant relatives gathered and caught up on each other's lives.

My first wedding. Sweet, but a little dull, RB thought, fluttering unseen through the crowd searching for something of interest. *Ah, this may be worthwhile,* she thought, closing in on a table of mostly well-endowed women.

Mandy left her place at the head table and waddled over to a group of women who were gathered at a table.

"Mandy! How are you? Oh, my gosh, I haven't seen you since, when? High School?"

"Hannah!" Mandy exclaimed, sitting down heavily in the chair next to her old school friend.

"My goodness, I barely recognized you. You look so… so, well, grown up!" Mandy responded, trying not to stare at Hannah's cleavage spilling out of her low-cut dress and practically resting on the table.

"Eyes up here," Hannah said, using two fingers to point at her own eyes.

Mandy felt a warm flush rise in her cheeks. "Um, sorry, your, uh, girls just kind of caught me off guard."

Hannah laughed as she sat back in her chair and arched her back. "Pretty impressive, huh? Got these babies as a gift from the ex." She smiled devilishly and cupped her breasts.

Good Lord! RB thought, gazing at the pudding-like mounds of flesh spilling out of Hannah's dress. *What the heck was that woman thinking! My gawd, I don't know if the alphabet goes high enough to give those casaba melons a bra size!*

Claire, who was seated across from Hannah, laughed. "Hi Mandy, how are you? I see you haven't heard about Hannah's, uh, enhancement."

"Um, no, been too busy getting ready for the baby I guess," Mandy said, gently rubbing her belly.

"Well, I see your ta-tas have been enjoying the side effects of pregnancy!" Hannah said, leaning forward and taking a sip of wine.

"Oh, my god, Hannah!" Claire spouted back, "The world does not revolve around the size of our boobs!"

"My bad. But seriously, Mandy, I don't remember you having such big hooters in high school!"

"Well, I didn't, and I can't say I am enjoying this. They hurt!"

"Yeah, right," Kate responded from across the table. "At first, when I was pregnant, I thought, whoo-hoo, I have boobies! But one day when I was, oh, I don't know, about six months preggers I opened a cabinet door, and well, it smacked me right in the boob! I thought, oh my god, that never happened before!" She grinned. "And next, the stretch marks came, and the whole breastfeeding thing made me feel like a total cow!"

"Oh, but girls," chimed in Jade who had been quietly absorbing the conversation, "breastfeeding is the best thing in the world you can do for your babies! And for yourself!"

Oh, lordy, RB thought, *thank God that's one thing I never had to worry about. Can you imagine if my lovely cups had to be shoved aside for some drooling mouth that would no doubt spit up and stain my cups!* RB shuddered at the thought, her straps vibrating as she fought to still the image.

"Jade, I plan to breastfeed my little one," Mandy said, continuing to run her hand in circles across her expanded belly. "Any tips or hints you can give me?"

"Well, have you been toughening up your nipples?"

"Oh, yeah," Kate said, "you better start tweaking those nips and getting them ready for blast-off! You think your titties are sore now, wait until your little sucking machine has a go at 'em night and day! My little Brandon put blisters on my nips he sucked so hard!"

"Now, Kate," Jade admonished, "don't go scaring her. Most women don't let their babies suckle twenty-four/seven."

"Hey, he was a hungry boy, and I was a tired mama. But seriously, Mandy, don't make the mistake I did and let him suckle non-stop. Your nipples will kill you until they get used to all that sucking."

"Wow, ladies," Hannah interjected, "don't think I'm ever gonna let any babies latch onto these girls!"

"But Hannah," Claire said, "I thought boob jobs made your nipples insensitive. However, I'm afraid you would suffocate a poor child with those hooters."

"Can you even breastfeed after a boob job?" Kate asked.

"Who cares?" Hannah said. "These girls are never getting near a baby's mouth, and as far as sensitivity goes, these girls are just fine. Now," Hannah said, pushing her chair back from the table and standing, "who needs a drink? I'm buying!"

"Drinks are free, Hannah," Kate wryly stated.

"Yeah, that's why I'm buying," Hannah said with a grin.

Hannah walked away from the table, and Mandy leaned forward as best as she could and whispered across the table to Claire, "What the heck? I mean, seriously, I understand some gals want bigger boobies, but what was she thinking? Her back has got to be killing her holding up all that weight!"

Kate laughed, "Yeah, my Aunt Dottie had a breast reduction for that exact reason. From what my mom says, she had huge hooters by the time she was thirteen!" She leaned back and looked at her own breasts. "I guess she got all the ta-ta genes."

"But Kate," Claire said, "didn't anyone ever tell you that anything over a mouthful is a waste?"

Kate picked up a napkin and attempted to throw it at Claire. "Always looking on the bright side, eh, Claire?"

"Well," Jade said, turning towards Mandy, "I do think it's easier for a baby to breastfeed with smaller breasts. Have you checked into the LaLeche League yet?"

"La-Le what?"

"LaLeche League, come on, your baby is almost due! Don't tell me you haven't heard of them?"

"Oh yeah, right, aren't they a bunch of fanatical breastfeeders?"

"Well, I think fanatical is too strong a word. They offer emotional support and tips to help make the whole thing easier. Like, I didn't know that rubbing lanolin on my breasts would help with the soreness. You better have some on hand. Oh, and I hadn't heard of nipple cups, and I didn't know about all the nursing bra options. Not to mention all the different kinds of breast pumps out there. It's a good resource, and you can join chat rooms on the web to talk with other women going through the same issues you are."

"Uh, I'm going to have issues?"

"You know what I mean, or at least you will once that baby comes." Jade grinned. "I am so glad you are going to nurse. It truly is a wonderful experience."

Wow, RB thought, listening to the conversation. *Lanolin, nipple cups, nursing bras! This conversation is making me sag!*

Jade continued, "You know, your body produces oxytocin when you nurse."

"Is that anything like oxycodone?" Claire asked, tapping her empty beer bottle. "Where the heck is Hannah anyway?"

"Oh, good grief, Claire, it's like a love hormone. It calms you, and I think it helps your uterus get back in shape quicker or something. I know it helps you lose weight. Heck, I think you burn something like five hundred calories a day making milk."

"Well, aren't you just the talking encyclopedia today," Claire responded, standing. "It appears that Miss Tits isn't getting our drinks. Guess I'll buy," she said with a grin, glancing around the table. "Orange juice for you, Mandy?"

"Sure, thanks," Mandy replied, turning her attention to Claire and grinning. "Miss Tits, eh?"

Claire put her finger to her lips, "Shhh, don't tell her I said that. She might smack me with 'em."

Mandy laughed before turning back to Jade. "I guess I should have been paying a little more attention to the pamphlets my doctor gave me. Thanks for the advice. I may be calling you once Reed arrives."

"Reed! What a neat name! So, it's a boy?"

"It sure is," Mandy replied, affectionately rubbing her belly. "Pete and I can't wait."

"Oh, lordy," Kate interrupted, "check it out," she said, pointing to the dance floor.

Mandy and Jade turned towards the dance floor just as Claire returned with their drinks. Setting the cups on the table, she turned to follow their gaze. The girls burst out in laughter watching Hannah doing the bump with a man they didn't recognize.

"My god!" Claire exclaimed. "Check out her jugs!"

The women tried to stifle their giggles as they watched Hannah's boobs bounce with every bump.

"Me thinks they are going to escape!" Claire said, sitting down and turning in her chair to get a better view.

"Oh Claire," Kate chimed in while raising her phone, "I gotta get a picture of this. Check it out. One or two more hip bumps and those ginormous puppies are free!"

"Put that thing away," Jade said, reaching out and putting her hand over Kate's phone. "She's just having some fun, but don't you think we should tell her she is just about to free Willy?"

"Free Willy, my ass!" Claire giggled, "When those things cut loose, that guy's willy is gonna wanna get loose!"

Oh, my! RB exclaimed, watching in fascination. *I'd kinda like to get a look at those girlies. I bet her nipples are as big as silver dollars! I can't imagine what they look like with all the skin stretched out to accommodate all that silicone or whatever the heck she had shoved in there.*

"Oh, darn," Kate said, lowering her phone and reaching inside her blouse to place it in her bra. "The music stopped just when I was gonna get a good look at those overgrown cantaloupes!"

Claire stared at Kate. "Did I just see you put your phone in your bra?"

"Uh, yeah, best phone holder around."

The girls turned to stare at Kate. Jade burst out laughing. "Oh my gosh, never would I have thought of that! But with this stick-on bra, I don't think it would work."

"What are you talking about?" Kate said, looking at Jade's breasts.

"A stick-on bra, you know, it sticks to your tits."

"What sticks to your tits?" Hannah asked, returning to the table.

"Jade's bra!" Kate replied with a raucous giggle.

"Can't wear a stick-on bra with these girls," Hannah said pointing to her breasts with her index fingers. "Duct tape and pasties, that's all I need!"

"Are you serious?"

"Nah, but I bet it would work."

"No way I'm putting duct tape on my girls!" Claire chimed in. "Can you imagine how much that would hurt pulling it off?"

RB listened in quiet amazement. *Duct tape? Pasties? I wonder if anyone really does that! I am sure glad my owner knew better. I cannot imagine that sticky, gooey tape residue staining my lovely cups! And putting a phone in me! Heavens, what an unsightly bulge it would create. Oh, my, what if it stretched me out! These girls are exhausting me!*

"Well, I think pulling off a stick-on bra would hurt too!" Kate interjected.

"The first few times I wore it, it did hurt pulling it off, but I got the hang of it. You just need to pull it off carefully,"

"The first few times? You mean you can wear them more than once? Doesn't the sticky stuff wear off?"

"Nah, you just wash the cups off with some warm soapy water, let 'em air dry, and wear it another fifty times or so."

"Bet they would play hell on a nipple ring," Hannah said, giving a sly smile in Claire's direction.

The girls turned to stare at Claire.

"What? I was in college, and FYI, it wasn't a ring, they were bars."

"Oh, my goodness!" Mandy proclaimed, "I really do need to get out more often! Seriously, you had your nipples pierced?"

"Yeah, the things we do when we're young," she grinned.

"I can't imagine! Didn't that hurt like hell?"

"Well, it sure didn't feel good, but no pain, no gain!"

"And pray tell, what did you gain by having your nipples pierced?"

"Why increased sexual pleasure, of course!" Claire said with a smile.

"If that's the case," Jade said with a sly grin, "why don't you still wear them?"

"Good question. Come to think of it; I don't know. I took 'em out one day and never put them back in."

"So," Mandy began, fighting to stifle a giggle, "if you were to breastfeed, would you like, uh, how do I say this? Would you have to be careful about drowning the baby, like, wouldn't the milk just kinda pour out?"

Jade laughed. "I don't think it works like that, Mandy."

"Oh, good grief," Claire said. "They grew shut in nothing flat. You can't even tell I ever had them."

"Nothing flat around here," Kate giggled, lifting her beer bottle and pointing it in Hannah's direction.

"Oh, you're just jealous," Hannah replied, draining her glass of wine. "Man, dancing made me thirsty! Who's getting the next round?"

"If I recall," Kate said, continuing to point her now empty beer bottle at Hannah, "you were on your way to get us all a drink when you ended up on the dance floor. Who was that guy? You two were looking mighty, uh, intimate out there."

"You call that intimate?" Hannah laughed, "Let me tell you about intimate!" You know Stan? The hottie with the body. Works at the car repair place on Sunnydale Lane?"

"I think this is my cue to go get you gals some drinks," Mandy interrupted. "This body is in no shape to listen to sex talk, and I think Reed needs a walk anyway," she said, gently patting her protruding belly. "Same drinks all around, ladies?"

"Yeah, sure," Claire said, scooting her chair closer to Hannah. "Now spill, Hannah, and don't leave out any details."

Mandy shook her head and smiled at the girls as she lifted her overloaded frame and headed to the bar. *Some things never changed,* she mused to herself, recalling Hannah's reputation in High School.

Wow! This party sure is getting interesting! Nipple rings? I bet they play havoc on a bra's tender lining. RB shivered. *I think I'll follow Mandy to the bar - this conversation might get too heated for even me!*

"Hey, Mandy!" Mandy turned her head to the sound of her sister Kendall's voice. "How are you holding up?"

"Oh, doing fine. Getting the girls a drink," she said, nodding towards her table. "Hannah is telling stories about one of her lascivious affairs."

"Oh, too funny," Kendall said, turning towards the group of ladies seated at her table. "You haven't lived until you have heard about Hannah's exploits."

Ella, seated across from Kendall, laughed. "Yeah, I saw her out there dancing. She can sure shake it, eh?"

Brenda smiled, "She came and talked to me before her boob job."

Marilynn chimed in, "Yeah, and you came to me before yours! The circle of life!"

Mandy's mouth dropped open as she looked from Marilyn to Brenda, her eyes rapidly scanning Brenda's chest before looking up to her eyes.

"Close your mouth, Mandy," Kendall admonished. "It's not attractive or polite."

Mandy rapidly closed her mouth as Brenda and Marilyn smiled. "No harm no foul," Brenda said as she stood. "Let me help you get those drinks. I'd like to get an up-close look at those jugs."

"Thanks! All of you should join us. I'm getting a real education over there."

Oh, goodie! RB said as she hovered nearby. *This should be interesting! Hmm, I wonder what they did with their old bras? I wonder if they replaced them with any fabulous red bras?*

***

"Well, would you look at what the cat brought in!" Claire exclaimed when the girls arrived at their table. "Pull up some chairs, ladies. We can squeeze you in."

Mandy and Brenda handed the girls their drinks while chairs were rearranged and everyone was seated. Brenda nodded towards Hannah, "See how you are, you come to me for advice and don't come around to show off the finished product? I see how you are," she joked.

"Well, you can see 'em now."

"I sure can! What the hell were you thinking?"

"I was thinking ahead more than you! Are you sure you really had a boob job?"

"You had a boob job?" Kate blurted out. "When?"

Claire leaned over the table and stared directly at Brenda's breasts. "I don't believe that," she said, reaching her hand towards Brenda's chest.

Quickly leaning back, Brenda yelled, "Whoa girl, no touchy, no feely! If you must know, yes, I had a slight enhancement. Just needed to perk the girls up a little, and as a bonus, I'm not lopsided anymore."

Claire pulled her hand back, took a long drink from her beer, and studied Brenda's chest.

"Hmm, I see. Perfectly symmetrical, but tell me, do your nips still give you pleasure?"

"Oh my god, Claire! I can't believe you just said that!" Jade said, turning in her seat and glaring at Claire.

"What? No harm, just some ladies talking, just trying to get all the facts. Been thinking about getting a boob job myself. Hannah says her nips still give her pleasure. Why she was just telling us about this thing Stan did with his tongue and..."

"Claire!" Jade interrupted. "TMI!"

"Hey, it wasn't my story. Just reinforcing the fact that not all nipples lose sensation. Now tell me, Brenda, how about your sensation?"

"If you must know, I have found that I need more, uh, how to say this delicately, um, more pressure to garner the same benefits as before."

"Garner the same benefits?" Claire laughed. "You're too much. Why don't you just say they need to be tweaked harder?"

THE RED BRA

Hannah laughed, "Oh my god, Claire. No filter on your mouth this evening, eh?"

"Well, come on, inquiring minds want to know. Tell us, Hannah, any downside to your big hooters?"

"Yeah, new bras are expensive!"

Duh, RB thought, pushing out her cups and lifting her straps. *No price is too high for beauty!*

"They sure are," Marilynn chimed.

"You had a boob job too?" Kate repeated for the second time in less than five minutes. "Anyone else here had a boob job I haven't heard about?"

The girls tittered as they glanced around the table, all eyes at bust level.

"Since we are all baring our souls, or should I say breasts, figuratively speaking that is," Marilynn began. "Yes, I had an enhancement done as a graduation gift to myself from college. And to answer the question that is sure to fall out of Claire's mouth at any second, yes, there has been some decrease in sensation to my nipples."

"Sorta sounds like Hannah's nips are the exception to the rule," Claire said.

"One thing I didn't like," Marilynn continued, "was how big my areolas got. Now, Brenda, I did warn you about that, but did you warn Hannah?"

"What's going on here?" Claire asked. "Is there some club I don't know about for the 'I wanna boob job' set?"

Ella, who had been sitting quietly nursing her beer spoke up. "If there is, can I join?"

"You want a boob job?" Kendall asked.

"Well," Ella said, leaning back in her chair, "I don't exactly fill out this bridesmaid dress, now do I?"

"Does Jerry know you want one?"

"Hell," Brenda interjected, "I didn't know you wanted one!"

"I didn't know I wanted one either," Ella laughed, "but I am beginning to feel like the minority over here. I wouldn't mind a little more bounce to the ounce."

"Well," Marilynn said, "not sure you're gonna get any bounce. These girls don't exactly move a whole lot. First time I had sex with these babies I had to be on top cuz when I was on the bottom these ladies stayed nice and perky and oh my god, did it hurt when John put all his weight on me!"

"I don't see how being on top is a downfall!" Claire said. "Another check for the plus side, or should I say plus size!"

"Funny girl," Brenda said. "But as you can see, I didn't go for the super-size, and I can still have sex in any position I want!"

"Well," Hannah, who had been uncharacteristically quiet said, "I did, and I have no regrets."

Whoa! The things I'm learning! RB thought. *But I'm usually tossed to the side during sex so how should I know such things!*

"Yeah," Ella said, "But how's that gonna work when it's time to start getting mammograms? Can they even spot cancer around all that silicon or whatever it is they use these days?"

"I'll be honest," Marilynn said, "I didn't even think about mammograms, or breast cancer, or any of that stuff when I had mine done. Hell, the ink wasn't even dry on my diploma when I went to the boob doctor. Gotta love all those credit cards I got while in college," she said, looking over at Hannah. "I didn't want to wait for a divorce settlement to get mine."

"Well, la-de-da," Hannah said. "You have a problem with how I paid for my tits? Oh, wait, you have to get married to get divorced."

"Zing!" Claire said, raising her beer bottle in a mock toast. "Let's stop all this tit for tat nonsense." Claire giggled, "Tit for tat, get it? Her grin widened. Now, tell us about your mammogram experiences, Hannah."

Hannah took a sip of wine and slowly put her glass down. She stared directly at Claire. "What makes you think I've had a mammogram? Good lord, I'm not forty!" She looked around the table. "Anyone over forty here?" Her voice rose as she continued. "Anyone had a stranger smash their tits?"

The table became quiet as everyone became preoccupied with their drinks. Hannah picked up her wine glass and drained it, slamming it on the table when she finished.

"Well," Kate began, "I know sometimes those machines bust open the implants. Pun intended," she grinned as she tried to add some levity to the conversation.

"Oh my god, really?" Jade inquired.

"Yeah, I have a cousin that it happened to. She had the saline kind. I guess she'd had them about ten years when suddenly she noticed one of her boobs getting smaller. The doctor told her it most likely happened during her mammo, which is why," Kate continued as she pointed her beer bottle one at a time towards each of the enhanced ladies, "you ladies should have an MRI instead. Especially you, Hannah."

"Duly noted," Hannah replied dryly, but I don't think this whole busting of boobs thing happens with the modern jobs."

"Oh, I don't know," Brenda said. "Mine are silicon, and my GYN said I should have the MRI instead of the squish kind. Not just because of the possibility of them busting, but because no matter what kind of implant you have there is always the possibility of an abnormality not showing up because of the implant."

"Guess I'll go with the MRI," Hannah said dryly while standing and picking up her empty wine glass and surveying the crowd of people. "Where's the happy couple? Come on girls, it's time to get our party on! This is a wedding, not a boob contest!"

"What are you talking about, boob contest? I don't see any wet t-shirts," Claire said, scooting her chair back and standing beside Hannah.

"My point, exactly," replied Hannah. "It's time to quit talking about our titties and get our groove on!" Hannah grabbed Claire's hand and pulled her out to the dance floor while waving at the other girls to join them.

"I better sit this one out," Mandy said as the ladies headed towards the dance floor. "I think I'll go find Pete. You gals boogie extra hard for me, okay?"

"Will do," Kate said, dancing her way towards the floor. "Oh, look, there's Jill and Todd!" Kate pointed towards the far side of the dance floor.

The girls danced towards them, then around them, until the entire group of people on the dance floor had encircled the couple. The band broke into "We are Family" as the dancers whooped and hollered, cajoling the couple to kiss in between loud bursts of singing along with the band.

RB delighted in the scene on the dance floor. *You ain't just a kidding,* she thought, listening to the girls sing. *They definitely have all their sisters with them, and then some.* She continued to flutter about the wedding while mulling over the things she had heard. *My, oh my, I don't get why all these ladies feel the need to enhance their breasts! But,* she thought, puffing out her well-endowed cups, *I guess if you've never had itty bitty titties one shouldn't judge. But all this talk about mammograms and breast cancer detection! Shouldn't these ladies be considering that before having a boob job? Seriously,* she continued to think as she fluttered outside the tent, *is their self-esteem so low they need bigger boobies to make them feel good about themselves? Oh, my, there I go, judging again. My bad. As they say, until you've bounced a mile in my cups, don't judge!*

Chapter 14
Hannah

annah rolled over on her side and looked at the clock beside her bed. 9:20 glowed in bright red numerals. *Oh, my god,* she thought, rolling on to her back and placing her arm over her pounding head. *I can't believe it's that late. I never sleep this late.* She pulled the sheet off her naked body and sat on the side of the bed. *Whoa, holy crap, I don't feel so hot.* Resting her head in her hands, she began to recall the previous evening. "What the hell did I do?" she moaned half out loud. Getting up, she stumbled to the bathroom, observing her clothes from the prior evening strewn from the bathroom towards her bed. *Jill and Todd's wedding. I was at Jill and Todd's wedding.* She sat on the toilet shaking her head. *Oh, god, I swore I would never drink that much again.* Slowly standing, she grabbed a robe that was hanging on the back of the bathroom door and wandered towards the front of her house. She looked out the window and saw her car parked in the driveway. *Geez, surely I didn't drive myself home drunk.* She sat down hard on the couch and tried to think. *Ok, I remember the wedding and sitting around with the girls talking about, about what? Oh, yeah, boobs. For god's sake, they act like no one ever got a major boob job. Like it's any of their business what I do with my body.* She glanced down at her chest and arched her back. *It will be a cold day in hell before I ever let them know about the back pain I now have. Besides, all I need to do is exercise to get my back muscles built up, and I'll be fine.* She sat and stared mindlessly into space while trying to ignore the throbbing pain in her head. *Okay, we danced. What else did I do?* She had flashes of dancing not only with the girls but with a guy. *Think, Hannah, when did you get so drunk?* Carefully rising from the couch, she slowly walked to the kitchen and began a pot of coffee. Staring mindlessly at the percolating pot, she vaguely remembered talking to Wally. *Was his wife around? God, I can't remember. Crap, I think I also talked to Erick. Did I flirt with every married man there? Why do I do that? Oh, yeah, I know why, because my husband left me for a man.* Wrapping her robe tightly around herself, she hugged herself hard while thinking back on her divorce. Her ex offered her a healthy settlement and alimony if she promised not to tell anyone about his sexual preferences. Before the divorce was final, he took off to parts unknown, and most people assumed he took up with another woman. *I'm glad he's in the closet,* she thought, hugging herself harder. *People can think whatever they want. Left me for a man, geez,* she thought, her mind wandering back to the previous night. "Oh, god," she moaned. *I think I did some shots.* Her mind flashed to a scene of herself at the bar with a group of people. *Who was I with? Did I shoot my big mouth off? Ok, calm down. This is just a serious case of hangover anxiety. It's never as bad as I think.* "Damn." She poured herself a mug of coffee and sat down at the kitchen table. *When am I ever going to learn?* she asked herself as she idly leafed through a pile of mail on the table. She picked up a sale flyer from Macy's, and an envelope that was partially stuck to the back fell to the table. Hannah looked at the return address. It was from Glendale Memorial. Her heart began to race as she fingered the envelope. *Oh, shit, I can't deal with this today,* she thought, tossing the envelope back on the table.

Hannah thought back to two years prior when she had her breast enhancement. She didn't like the word augmentation. She felt enhanced, not augmented. She gave a wry smile thinking about the extremely generous check her ex had given her as hush money, but she did wish he could see what some of his money bought her. "Ha," she laughed out loud as she thought to herself, *like these luscious babies would turn his head. How could I have been so stupid? He sure acted like he liked sex with me. At least in the beginning. At least I thought so. Shit, I don't know.* Picking up her coffee mug, she sipped the steaming java. *You would think after two and a half years I'd quit rehashing that.* Putting her coffee mug down, she reached inside her robe with her left hand and probed at the tissue underneath her right armpit close to her breast. She gently probed down to the side of her breast. Her middle finger found the hard lump, and she paused for a second before her index finger joined in as she gently felt around it. She removed her hand; satisfied nothing had changed since she last checked it. *And when was that?* she mused. *Seriously, what is wrong with you? If you had half a brain, you would check it every day, and you would open that damn envelope. Why didn't I go ahead and get a mammogram before my enhancement? Oh, yeah, because they said at my age, it wasn't really necessary, but I could get one if I wanted to. Wanted to? I've spent enough time listening to my mother and her friends talk about those boob crushers. Why would I put myself through that? There's no history of breast cancer in our family. I've always been healthy. For crying out loud, I eat frickin' blueberries every day. Aren't they supposed to keep shit from attacking shit in your body?*

She picked up her coffee cup and held the now tepid mug tightly in her hands attempting to stop the trembling dance her fingers were itching to perform. She tapped her bare foot on the floor and slowly rocked back and forth to a soundless rhythm that echoed through her brain. "I'll be okay, I'll be okay, it's all going to be okay, nothing's wrong, I'll be okay, I'll be okay."

RB's straps dropped and hung below her cups as she witnessed the ongoing litany of words being spoken over and over in a monotonous tone that appeared to be a mantra of hope for Hannah. *Open the damn envelope, open the damn envelope!* RB pushed her thoughts through the air, willing Hannah to open the envelope and hopefully discover all her brooding was for naught, and if it wasn't, well, she would just have to deal with it.

Hannah's rocking slowed, and she gently placed her mug on the table as her toe-tapping ceased. Wiping a lone tear from her cheek, she sat up straight. "I can handle this. I really can. I can handle this," she spoke softly, turning her head to face the morning light shining in through the window. "I can handle this," she spoke louder as she picked up the envelope and ran her finger lightly over her name. She tapped the envelope on the table repeatedly then threw it back amongst the sale flyers. "Screw it. I need a shower and more sleep. I feel like hell."

Walking into the bathroom, Hannah remembered the conversation at the wedding about mammograms. "It's none of their damn business," she muttered under her breath while removing her robe and bending over the tub to turn on the water. "Ohh!" she yelped, startled as her breasts landed on the side of the tub, their cold porcelain causing her nipples to instantly become erect. She fell back and landed with a thud on the floor. Pulling her knees up to her chest and wrapping her arms around her legs she sat, leaning against the door. Tears began to fall in a thunderous downpour, her heart aching with regret as she thought of all the things she had yet to accomplish in her life. Her sobs turned to hiccups, and she reached up towards the sink and pulled a washcloth down and ran it over her tear stained face. *Get a grip, girl,* she thought to herself. *You haven't even looked at the damn envelope yet. You're over-reacting. It's probably just scar tissue from the enhancement or something.* Hannah stood and leaned on the sink to steady herself. "Damn, this is one hell of a hangover," she said out loud to herself in the mirror. "You look like hell." She stared intently at herself, looking deep into her own eyes. "Who are you? You really screwed up last night; you know that, don't you? And why did you get so drunk? Geez, get over it." She stood up straight and marched naked into the kitchen and picked up the envelope. Without pausing, she ripped it open and quickly scanned the contents. *The results of your sonogram were highly suggestive of malignancy.* The words bounced off the page and reverberated through her brain. Highly suggestive of malignancy. The words repeated themselves over and over in her mind, seemingly caught in an echo chamber from where there was no release. She dropped the envelope and walked slowly back to the bathroom. Wrapping a towel around her breasts, she once again leaned over the tub and turned on the water. She had a feeling of being disconnected from her body as she stepped into the shower and let the water rain over her body. She stood still, her eyes vacant as her mind slowly tried to wrap itself around the atrocity that had invaded her.

THE RED BRA

Oh no, no, no..... RB wailed. She lifted her cups, straightened her straps, and flew off into the morning sky. She flew as high as she could, heading towards the warmth of the sun, its beams shining down and warming the coldness that had overtaken her. *This can't be happening. This just can't be happening. That poor girl, hasn't she had enough thrown at her?* RB dropped her straps and became entrenched in a thermal, allowing her to be at the mercy of the universe.

Time ceased to have all meaning as RB floated from day to night and back again. Over and over again she watched the sun rise and set. Her once shiny satin straps became tattered as the winds whipped them to and fro. She thought back on all she had witnessed through her stint with the freedom that came from being disconnected from all earthly boundaries. She reflected back to her time observing Riley and wondered if she had since passed the pencil test. Her weary straps gave a slight shimmy, recalling how vibrant and resilient Riley was. *But that mother. Hmpf! Laura! Now she is something else. Come to think of it though, she does remind me of someone. Hmm, it's right on the tip of my...* she bounced her cups and jiggled, *my... oh never mind.*

RB looked across the vast sky. Her mood grew pensive while watching the sun dip lower towards the horizon. She began to drift closer to land before pausing to hover amidst the clouds while debating where to go next.

Briefly, she thought back to Hannah and the uncertainty that her future held before her thoughts jumped to Derrick and Jessica. She gave a quick shimmy thinking of their young love and felt certain it would continue to blossom. She puffed out her cups, remembering watching Derrick, his brother Darnell, his mother, Emma, and father, Charles sitting around the dining table after church. Emma. RB straightened her straps, thinking of the matriarch of the family. *She is one strong woman. I would imagine Derrick is off to college by now. I bet that's hard on Emma since, after all, he is the baby of the family. Hopefully, by now, she and Charles have passed most of the farming duties to Darnell, and they get to travel and visit their son, Tim and their grandsons, Jerry and James. I know she was just devastated when Tim moved to California.*

WAIT A SECOND! RB shouted unheard through the misty clouds. She pushed her cups out, raised her straps straight up and paused in mid-flight. *Jerry! OMG! He was Todd's roommate and best man at the wedding. How did I not realize that!* She jiggled her cups, tilted back, and laughed with total abandonment and glee for the first time in several years. RB paused as the realization struck her that she had no idea how many times the seasons had come and gone since she left Hannah. *Just how long have I been drifting aimlessly through this purgatory? Why have I allowed myself to be mindless for so long? Oh, yeah,* RB dropped her straps. *Hannah. I really shouldn't have turned my straps on her.*

Continuing to think back, RB hoped Missy had learned her lesson and had once and for all quit showing off her ta-tas. *At least now she has some bras that fit*, RB wryly thought before her thoughts landed back to Hannah and the uncertainty that her future held. *I can't keep turning my straps on her,* RB thought, shaking herself in an attempt to perk up her sagging cups. *Cancer, smancer! She's young and vibrant. I cannot give up on her!* With that thought, RB dropped lower and sailed off in search of Hannah.

Chapter 15
Support

RB sailed along the western coast enjoying the cool sea breezes and not minding the salty spray that occasionally polka dotted her cups with their watery brine. Turning inland, she spotted Hannah and Jill walking into a stately building with the word, HOPE, boldly embossed across the archway to the main door. Hannah's long blond hair was replaced by a short bob that hung askew on her head. Her blouse hung loosely, no longer protruding outward with the pressure of her voluptuous breasts stuffed inside like one too many acorns in a chipmunk's cheeks. RB's weathered straps sagged while watching them enter the building.

Oh, my, how long have I been gone? RB thought, following the unlikely couple into the building and through a door that bore an embossed sign stating *Support Group*.

RB briefly considered the permanence of the sign, indicating many had come for support prior, and many would come in the future. Following the women, she briefly wondered how their friendship had evolved to such closeness that Jill was accompanying Hannah to her support group. *Support Group, gotta love that name,* RB nervously laughed, lifted her weathered cups and gave a brief shimmy. *I never thought there would be a time when I would feel like this, but I definitely need a little more support. Not only is my physical being in dire need of repair, but my soul is getting weary. I can't believe how worn my entire essence has become! But on a happier note, I am glad Hannah and Jill are close. I am sure she has needed someone to be there for her.*

"Thank you so much for coming with me, Jill," Hannah said as they made their way to a table containing an array of juices and fresh fruit.

"Oh, Hannah, you know I don't mind," Jill said, gently squeezing Hannah's arm. "I'm glad you came to my wedding, and we reconnected. You know, we did have some fun times in high school. You always made the world seem; I don't know, brighter."

"Really?" Hannah had a surprised look on her face as she turned to look at Jill. "I had the feeling you thought I was loud and obnoxious."

"Well," Jill grinned, "at times you were a little bit of both, but that made you exciting. I'll tell you a little secret. I always wished I could be more like you. Ya know, not afraid to say what you thought and able to walk up to cute guys you didn't know and just start talking."

Hannah stared at Jill, her mouth dropping open in a speechless O.

"Well, I'll be a monkey's uncle! Hannah Lee Kane, I don't believe I have ever seen you speechless!"

Hannah closed her mouth and cleared her throat while reaching for the orange juice. "You think they have any vodka to mix in here and spice this party up a little?"

"See what I mean," Jill grinned, "always the one looking to liven things up a bit."

"Did I hear vodka?" a lady's voice behind Jill questioned. "I thought this was wine country. Where's the wine?"

"Oh, my friend here," Jill said, waving her arm towards Hannah, "was lamenting the fact they didn't have any vodka."

Hannah looked at the lady and observed the bandanna wrapped tightly around her head. She was thin and wore baggy jean capris and a Hard Rock Café t-shirt. She had a large rose tattoo above her ankle, and her feet bore black plastic flip-flops. As her eyes continued their downward trek, she noticed that she appeared to have had a recent pedicure, complete with a large pink rhinestone on each big toe.

"So, you like my rhinestones? It gives people something to look at besides my bald head," she laughed. Name's Laura; this here is my big sis, Joan. She flew us out here so I could go to that fancy cancer center they got here. She's the best." She smiled at her sister. "Even got us a condo with an ocean view. Sure is nice to have a rich sister."

"It's a timeshare," Joan interjected, reaching out her hand while giving a sour look to her sister.

"Nice to meet you, Joan." Hannah grinned while accepting her handshake. "And nice to meet you, too, Laura. I'm Hannah, as in be by banana, Hannah fanna bonana, and this is my good friend, Jill. You sound like my kind of gal, Laura! You'd think they'd have a little something to help us with our anxiety, right? This is my first time here, and I'm not sure about sitting around telling a bunch of strangers about my hairless, puking, boob-less self."

"Come on Hannah," Jill interjected, "you're not boob-less."

"Look at this," Hannah said, pointing her hands towards her breasts. "These are not exactly the boobalicious babies I had before."

"Yes, they are, Hannah, they're your before before boobies."

Laura looked at Jill with a puzzled look, "Did you really just say before before boobies? And Hannah, did you actually say boobalicious babies? Good thing we're not drinking, or I'm not sure I could have said that!" she laughed. "I love it, boobalicious babies. So, tell me, what are boobalicious and before before boobies?"

Hannah laughed, and Jill shook her head. "I had some ginormous hooters installed shortly after my divorce. They were outstanding," she grinned. "Those were the boobalicious babies. That was before cancer reared its ugly head and wallah, back to the original, or the before before boobies. My triple B's. Lucky for me, I got to keep 'em." She leaned over and whispered in Laura's ear.

"Truthfully, it was a bit of a relief. Those things were killing my back and bruising my knees," she laughed and stood up. "Just kidding about the knees," she said with a wink. "Nice to meet you, Laura," Hannah said, grabbing Jill's elbow. "We're going to go find a seat. Catch ya later."

Well how about that, RB thought. *Hannah certainly isn't the blubbering mess I last saw! Good for her! I knew she'd get her old self back.* RB fluttered her straps in glee, watching Hannah and Jill locate a place to sit. RB turned her attention back to Joan. *Hmm, she sure looks familiar.* She swooped in for a closer look. *Oh, my goodness! That's Joan Browne! That's Carolyn's mom! What a small world. No wonder she looked familiar! I can't believe it!* RB clapped her straps together in excitement. *Goody, goody! Wait a minute, isn't that also Riley's mom, Laura? How did I forget her? How long have I been gone! Laura and Joan are sisters? Laura has the big C! How can this be? Poor Riley. I shouldn't have left her!*

Laura turned towards Joan, "Wow, that Hannah's a hoot, huh? Boobalicious," she laughed. "Gotta love her sense of humor," she said, pouring herself a glass of orange juice. "But she's right, ya know, a *real* drink could sure make this easier."

"You know you shouldn't drink alcohol while on chemo, right?"

Laura glared at Joan. "Are you really going to lecture me now? I don't need this crap from you." Quickly, she turned her back on Joan, bumping the table in the process. Her cup toppled over, and juice poured over the white plastic tablecloth that was littered with tiny pink metallic ribbons. Laura, oblivious to the sticky orange liquid making its way towards the neatly splayed out napkins, headed to the restroom.

Joan watched the rivulets formed by the running juice, pink ribbons floating in their midst, as it traveled around the napkins edges before beginning to cascade down the side of the tablecloth. *Really? Really?* she thought to herself. *I'm just looking out for her best interest, and as usual, nothing I say is right in her eyes.* She lifted the edge of the tablecloth attempting to keep the juice contained when a young man sporting a long black ponytail quickly scooped up the napkins, rescuing them from their impending doom.

"Here, let me help you with that," he said, quickly grabbing the sodden napkins and deftly stopping the waterfall from continuing its sticky path to the linoleum below.

"Oh, thank you so much. You look like you've had some experience cleaning up messes."

He smiled and used his free hand to push his black frame glasses up higher on his nose. "I spent some time as a busboy."

"And don't forget helping me out with the little ones," an older woman wearing a turquoise scarf stylishly wrapped around her head interjected. "Hello, I'm Emma Murphy, this here is my grandson, Jerry."

Jerry reached out a hand to Joan. Joan grasped his hand, let out a yelp, and quickly pulled her hand away.

"Oh man, I'm so sorry. I guess I don't know my own strength."

Joan laughed and looked at her hand. "I'm sure you are strong, but I believe this little thing," she said, plucking a metallic pink ribbon from her hand, "was the source of my rudeness. It must have stuck to your hand when you were sopping up the mess. Sharp little edges on these things, but no harm. Nice to meet you, Jerry, shall we try again?" Joan said, once again reaching out her hand.

Hearing the commotion behind her, Jill turned in her seat. *I recognize that voice,* she thought to herself. "Excuse me for a minute," she said, turning back to face Hannah. "I think that's Jerry over there. You remember him, don't you? He was Todd's best man at the wedding."

Oh geez, Hannah thought to herself. *Just what I need, another reminder of that day. But seeing as I really don't remember that day, que sera sera. I just hope I didn't hit on him.*

"Yeah, I remember him. He gave a wonderful toast and all that, right?"

"Uh, right," Jill said, rising from her seat and giving Hannah a puzzled look.

Surely he gave a toast, best man and all, Hannah thought while reaching her hands up to check that her wig was on straight.

"Jerry?" Jill queried as she made her way towards him.

Jerry turned at the sound of his name. "Jill, oh my gosh, how are you? I don't think I've seen you since the wedding. Sorry about that, I keep meaning to call Todd and see if he's up for some one on one time on the basketball courts, but," his voice faltered as the reality of where he was struck him. His face fell, and he looked to the ground for a moment before slowly raising his head and looking Jill in the eyes. "Jill, I didn't know. Is Todd here? Why didn't he tell me?" He grabbed her hand.

"But," Jill began to speak.

"No, there's no buts. I'm here with my Grandma Em." He turned to introduce her only to see her hastily walking away in the direction of the ladies' room.

"She insisted on getting some wet paper towels," Joan said with a shrug, continuing to move the platters of food away from the spilled juice that continued to travel across the table.

Turning back to Jill, Jerry continued, "She's got stage III. She's staying with dad, and he's taking care of her while she undergoes treatment. Since Grandpa Charlie died, she's been lost. Of course, she still has Derrick at home and all but, well, oh my gosh, I'm rambling. I'm so sorry, what stage is your cancer? You look great. Sorry, that didn't come out right."

"Chill, Jerry, I'm okay. I'm here to support my friend, Hannah," she said, turning her head and pointing out Hannah, who was engrossed in a conversation with the lady seated next to her.

Jerry grabbed Jill and gave her a quick hug. "You scared the bejeesus out of me! Thank God you're okay, but uh, sorry about your friend."

"Thanks, I'm just glad I can be here for her, and how wonderful of you to come with your grandma. Is that her?" Jill asked, acknowledging the elderly woman who was quickly approaching them, her hands filled with sopping wet paper towels.

"It sure is," Jerry said, reaching out and gently taking his grandmother by the arm and escorting her to where Jill was standing.

"Now Jerry, you don't need to coddle me," Emma said, patting Jerry on the arm and dripping water from the paper towels on his sleeve. "I need to help Joan clean up the juice."

Joan walked over and reached for the towels. "Here, let me take care of that. It will just take a second."

"Very well, dear," Emma said, relinquishing her hold on the paper towels and turning her attention back to Jerry.

"Grandma, I'd like you to meet my friend, Jill. I was the best man at her wedding."

"Pleased to meet you, Jill. I'm glad you could be here."

"Oh, she's not sick," Jerry blurted out. "Her friend is. Oh, crap, I'm sorry, Jill."

Jill touched Jerry on the arm. "Jerry, it's okay."

Emma smiled at Jill. "I didn't think you were ill, my dear. Jerry's dad, Tim, usually comes with me, and I think all these ladies with their lovely headpieces befuddle Jerry," she said, reaching up and touching her scarf while giving Jill a wink. "It looks like they have a full house today. It's such a wonderful group of people. I'm sure your friend will find solace within the group. I know I have." She looked up at Jerry, "I think we should go sit down. Nice to meet you, Joan," she said with a smile before turning to make their way to their seats.

"Yes, and I better get back to Hannah," Jill said. "I'll catch up with you later, Jer. Nice to meet you, Mrs. Murphy."

You have got to be kidding me! Has this cancer invaded all my new acquaintances? Good lord, am I somehow responsible for this? It seems everywhere I went, someone was stricken with breast cancer. Breast cancer! The reason for my being, the most delicious part of the female anatomy! Hannah, Laura, and now Emma! Poor Derrick, I had no idea his father died, and now his mother has cancer? What in the heck is this world coming to? I sure hope he and Jessica are still together. I must check on them, but I'm incredibly tired. I can barely raise my straps. Her ragged straps drooped, and her faded cups sagged while she thought about the people she had come to care about, and how they were all connected by the disease that had taken over her reason for being. Breasts. Lovely breasts.

***

Joan absentmindedly rubbed her hand back and forth on the table while staring with blank eyes at the bathroom door where Laura had escaped. *My sweet Rebecca,* Joan thought, remembering her free-spirited daughter. *How she begged Jeff and me to let her go to the University of California. If only she had gone to the local community college for two years like I wanted she would still be with us.* Being in California, and so close to the place of Rebecca's death filled Joan with unspeakable sadness. She knew she was adept at putting up a good front for her friends and family, but sometimes the depth of her despair was almost too much to bear. Having Carolyn still at home was her saving grace, and now, having Laura to care for gave her another focus. *Thank God Jeff and I have the funds to get her out here to California*, she thought. *Plus, I can keep an eye on her.* Joan thought back to Laura's initial phone call to tell her she had cancer. She was loaded and slurring her words. Poor Riley caught the brunt of her mother's anger at being poisoned with cancer. As much as it saddened her, Laura knew Riley was much better off staying with her father, Joel, while her mother fought her battle with cancer, and ultimately, alcohol.

Feeling a hand on her shoulder, Joan was interrupted from her reverie. Startled, she jumped and saw Laura, a sheepish grin erupting on her hollow face.

"Where'd you come from? I thought you were in the bathroom?"

"I was, but when I came out, you were busy talking to people, so I went outside to sit for a bit. They have such a peaceful flower garden out back. Did you know you can see the ocean from there? I feel better. Sorry for snapping at you, I know you just want to help." Reaching out, she embraced her sister in a warm hug.

"I love you, sis, you know that, don't you?" Joan said. "I just want you to get well. I couldn't bear it if you, you, you know, if..."

"Shush, don't even say it. This cancer crap is not going to get the best of me. Now let's go find a seat. It looks like they have already begun."

Joan and Laura took a seat, and the moderator smiled at them.

"Welcome, ladies. We are finishing up with our introductions. Feel free to say as little or as much as you want. I'm Candace, and I've been cancer-free for six years." Her smile broadened. "Who would like to introduce themselves next?"

The motley group looked around the circle at each other. Some were smiling politely, and a few had stoic faces. Hannah silently dabbed at a stray tear that was sliding down her cheek while Emma absentmindedly spun her wedding ring in circles.

"Well," Emma began, raising her head and releasing the grasp on her ring. "Guess I might as well introduce myself to those of you who do not know me." She looked around the room smiling and nodded in recognition to those she knew from prior meetings. "My name is Emma Murphy, and this here," she said, turning slightly to look at Jerry and patting him on the knee, "is my grandson, Jerry. I married a farmer, God rest his soul, when I was barely twenty years old. But I won't bore you with the details of life on the farm. I was diagnosed with breast cancer a little over a year ago. I wasn't one to go to the doctor much and to be honest, I had no desire to have some machine squash my breasts. I was always busy with the farm and the family, and frankly, I never thought about checking my breasts for lumps or even going to the doctor for a check-up. Like I said, I didn't much fancy going to the doctor. When my husband, Charles, passed I lost a bit of weight, and ladies, you know how it is," she paused and smiled at the group. "Weight always seems to go from the breasts first." There was a low murmur of giggles and a few nods of the head amongst the women. "That's how I noticed the lump. Without the extra padding, so to speak, it was kind of hard not to miss." Pausing for a moment, she looked down at her hands. She noted a softness to them that she hadn't seen in many years. She was used to seeing calluses formed by years of gardening and caring for livestock, crops, and children. Sighing, she held her hands out, palms down. Her nails were unpolished, short and neatly filed. Her right thumb was bent slightly outward; a sign of arthritis that was slowly working its way through her well-used body. "You know," she began, "this is the first time in many, many years I recall having soft hands. It seems foreign to me because as a farm gal my hands were always busy. Now," she continued, her voice growing softer, "my hands are soft, and my nails are clean." She looked around the room at the women watching her speak. She sat up straight and splayed her hands out on her knees. The light shining through the window ricocheted off her wedding ring. She smiled. "For every hardship, there's a blessing. If Charles were still alive, I would still be busty, and perhaps not noticed the lump until it was too late. If not for cancer, I wouldn't be here in California spending time with my son and my grandson." Turning to face Jerry, her smile broadened. "And I wouldn't have soft hands."

Laura broke the ensuing silence. "What stage were you in when you were diagnosed?"

Joan lightly elbowed Laura as several of the cancer-stricken women looked at her slightly appalled.

"As I said at the beginning of the meeting," Candace interrupted, "and as is noted in the pamphlets that were placed on your chairs, we don't ask questions of one another unless one asks for questions."

"My bad," Laura said, scooting to the side of her chair and noting that in her haste to join the already convened group she had not noticed the pamphlet and was sitting on it. "I'm sorry, I didn't mean any harm."

"No worries," Emma replied. "I was stage III at the time of my diagnosis."

"Oh, I'm sorry," Laura said, realizing just how far she had inserted her foot in her mouth.

"Don't be. I'm doing fine. I had chemo. They were trying to shrink the tumor enough to allow them to perform breast-conserving surgery, but it wasn't meant to be. I had a double mastectomy, and for those who are wondering, I chose not to have breast reconstructive surgery. What a relief not to have to wear a bra anymore!" She laughed. "Believe it or not, I was one of those bra-burning gals in the sixties. Of course, I did that as part of the cause, but truthfully, I always hated wearing those over the shoulder boulder holders. But I do have a few of those bras with the fake breasts to wear when I go out," she said, pushing her shoulders back so they could see that she did appear to have breasts.

"I guess I was one of the lucky ones," a petite lady sitting across from Laura commented. "I was at stage I when I was diagnosed and only needed a lumpectomy and radiation. I will say however, radiation made my cancer-stricken breast quite perky!" Several of the women laughed and nodded in agreement.

"Yeah," a brunette with long black hair pulled back in a ponytail commented, "I kidded with my doctor about giving a few shots of the big R to my other breast, so it would also be perky."

"No, you didn't!" a woman who appeared to be in her mid-forties blurted out.

"Sure did," she responded with a broad smile. "I'm a bit like Emma. I figured I could either wallow in my grief and do the poor me routine, or I could find something positive about the whole mess. True, my cancer was in an early stage, so I guess those of you who are in the later stages might think it's easy for me to say, but cancer is cancer. No matter what the stage. Kudos to Emma for looking for the positive side of all her hardships!"

Hannah had been sitting quietly and taking in the conversations around her. As she continued to listen to the women share their stories of hope and hearing how many had discovered a silver lining within their misfortune she began to realize just how much she had to be thankful for.

Candace stood, breaking Hannah from her thoughts. "Thank you all for coming today. I know it takes a lot of strength to share your feelings with others. Before we go, please stand, and if you are comfortable with it, grasp the hands of those on either side of you." As everyone stood and held hands, Candace looked slowly and purposefully at each person present. Remember, she began; you are bountiful, blissful, and beautiful. Repeat after me. I am bountiful, blissful, and beautiful."

"I am bountiful, blissful, and beautiful," the group chorused.

Candace smiled a genuine smile at each person present before releasing her hands from those next to her. "Feel free to stay as long as you want. The patio out back is open. Help yourself to the fruit and juice."

The group slowly broke away from their circle, and those acquainted with one another began their own conversations. Hannah maintained her grasp on Jill's hand and gave a gentle squeeze. "Thank you so much for suggesting this place and for bringing me here. You're a true friend, and I am grateful you are in my life. I think I have things in better perspective now."

"Oh, Hannah, you are so welcome. This was an eye-opener for me, too. How about that Emma, huh? I thought Jerry was going to die when she began talking openly about her breasts and her bra-burning days!"

"Yeah, she's something all right. Hey, do you think they would want to hang out for a while? It wouldn't hurt me to absorb a little more of Emma's positive energy!"

"That's a great idea, and I'd love to do some more catching up with Jerry," Jill said, scanning the room. "There's Emma, let's go ask."

Weaving their way through the crowd, they approached Emma standing near the refreshments talking to Laura. Jerry appeared at Emma's side balancing two plates filled with kiwi, blueberries, and papaya.

"Looks delicious!" Jill proclaimed. "I was hoping you two were going to stick around for a bit. Would you like to join us and sit outside? You, too, uh - Laura, right?" she said, nodding in her direction.

"Yeah, I'm Laura, the one with her foot in her mouth."

"Now, now," Emma said, looking at Laura while freeing Jerry's hand from a plate of fruit. "You asked an honest question, no harm done. Please, join us."

"It is beautiful out back," Laura said, lowering her head and examining the rhinestone on her right toe. "That's why I didn't hear the rules of the group. I was sitting on the patio feeling sorry for myself, but I must say," she continued, raising her head and making eye contact with Emma, "you have helped me put things in perspective.

"One thing I have learned throughout the trials and tribulations of my life is that if I think happy, I will be happy."

"Oh, Emma, I love your attitude. I could sure use more happy thoughts. I'd love to stay and chat? Let me see if my sister, Joan, would like to stay for a bit."

"I met Joan," Jerry said, before tossing another blueberry into his mouth. "I helped her with an OJ mishap before the meeting."

"That would have been my doing," Laura said while looking over his shoulder and scanning the room. "Sorry about that, but where in the heck did Joan go?" "Oh, there she is," she said, waving her hand in the air.

Joan made her way over and smiled at Jerry and Emma. "I see you've met my sister."

"Yes, we have," said Jerry. "We were talking about sitting out back for a bit."

"That would be nice. Laura told me how peaceful it is."

RB struggled to follow the group to the patio. *What's happening to me?* she wondered as she fluttered haphazardly in the gentle breeze and landed in a nearby hibiscus bush, its red flowers creating a nest for her faded and worn being.

Taking a seat, Joan fumbled through her purse and pulled out a tattered tissue. She dabbed the corner of her eyes.

"What's wrong, dear?" Emma inquired, placing her hand on her knee.

"Oh, nothing," she quietly said as a tear slipped down her cheek.

Laura, who was watching her sister, spoke up. "Maybe," she softly said, "it would help if you talked about it."

"Perhaps," Joan began, "but you all don't need to hear about my sorrow."

"It's okay," Laura said. "I know I've been so wrapped up in my own problems that I haven't been there for you like I should."

"Oh Laura, you've helped me more than you know."

"But coming back to California and all," her voice trailed off.

"Rebecca loved California," Joan began. She looked at Emma then looked at the expectant faces around her. "Rebecca is my oldest daughter." Lowering her head, she whispered quietly, "Was my oldest daughter. Our dear, sweet, Becca. She begged her father and me to let her go to school in California. We spent many summers here. She loved the ocean and the glamour of Hollywood." Pausing for a few seconds, she fumbled with the wadded-up tissue before raising her head and smiling. "She was stunning and so talented. She was on the cheerleading squad at UCLA. I was crazy happy when she made the squad. She did go through a bit of a 'wild child' stage when she was in high school, and I felt being on the college squad would help to keep her grounded." Joan looked at the ground and kicked at a red hibiscus flower, its spent and tattered petals lying lifeless at her feet. Continuing to talk, she kept her eyes peeled on the petals. It was New Year's Eve, and she and a group of friends were going to a party at a hotel in Santa Barbara. It was her first New Year's Eve at the legal drinking age. She was so excited when she called to tell me what she was doing. She texted me a picture of the red blouse she had purchased for the occasion. It was beautiful." Pausing, she looked up to the cloudless sky before continuing. "It was a deep red with delicate silver sparkles sprinkled throughout. I remember her excitement when she told me about the red bra she found that had a silver lining in the cups. She said it was meant to be hers. I keep telling myself there's a reason for everything, but that red bra, that damn red bra," she said, choking back tears. "When they arrived at the hotel the bellhop took her blouse from the trunk. From what I understand, she had looped the bra over the hanger with her blouse and laid it on top of her suitcase. Anyway," she sighed, "when the bellhop hooked it to his cart a gust of wind grabbed the bra, and it was fluttering in the breeze. Rebecca ran and reached for the hanger. I guess she was embarrassed that her bra was dancing in the wind, but frankly," she paused, looking up at the solemn faces, "I didn't think my Rebecca Browne embarrassed easily."

RB, camouflaged by the red hibiscus flowers quivered. She felt her straps twinge ever so slightly as their tattered edges healed and became whole. Her cups shook, regaining their former brightness, and their silver lining expanded and rimmed the outer edges of her cups.

Joan continued, "When she grabbed the hanger, the bra flew off, and she chased after it. She ran into the path of a car turning into the hotel. It wasn't going fast, but it knocked her to the ground. She hit her head, and well," rapidly blinking her eyes she looked down, and her red-rimmed eyes dropped tears to the ground. "They said she died instantly." Joan wrapped her arms around herself as a sudden warm breeze filled with the scent of the salty ocean and hibiscus flowers sailed through the patio. She glanced towards the nearby hibiscus bush as the breeze danced around the flowers. "Oh my God!" she gasped as her hands flew to her head and slowly slid down each side of her face while she stared, mouth agape, at the bush. The others followed her gaze and were bewildered at what they saw.

RB, overcome by her transformation and by the revelation she had just witnessed, looked at Joan, then looked towards the bright light that was shining down on her and beckoning her to follow. *Mom,* Rebecca Browne thought as the realization struck her that she truly was no longer encased in the melons of her past. *Mom, I'm okay,*

THE RED BRA

I'm really okay. Her inner voice faded, and she followed the light, leaving the red bra behind.

ABOUT THE AUTHOR

Jenny Middleton taught English and science to middle school students for over two decades. She is the recipient of several teaching awards, including the prestigious Milken Educator Award. She enjoys traveling throughout the United States in her motorhome and is inspired by the beauty of nature.

To learn more about Jenny visit:

www.jennymiddleton.com

Twitter @ jmiddle758

Instagram @jmiddle758

Email: jenny.middleton.rb@gmail.com

Other Books
by Jenny Middleton

Who Is Big? Written for the early reader, *Who Is Big* sees the world through the eyes of an ant who happily proclaims to be the biggest of all creatures. Readers delight in predicting what creature will appear next as they rhyme their way through the various animals. The changes in the ant's state of mind open communication about happiness. Additional facts comparing and contrasting the animals foster discussion between the beginning and advanced reader.

Available at Amazon.com